Haunts and Howls Collections

Haunts and Howls and Guardian Spells
Haunts and Howls Where Demons Dwell

HAUNTS AND HOWLS WHERE DEMONS DWELL

A CONTEMPORARY FANTASY COLLECTION

KAT SIMONS

HAUNTS AND HOWLS WHERE DEMONS DWELL

CONTENTS

INTRODUCTION

In 2021, I published a collection of contemporary fantasy stories called Haunts and Howls and Guardian Spells, in which I had five stories all tied into a theme of Guardians and Protectors, with a spooky twist. I had so much fun with that collection, I decided to write another one in a similar vein—with Haunts and Howls—but with a different theme. The stories that rolled out of me determined the theme. And that theme turned out to be Demons.

I can't help but wonder if there wasn't some underlying, Freudian meaning to that, given the year that was in it.

Or maybe I just like spooky stories with demons in them.

I have two different urban fantasy series that feature demons quite prominently. One, the Cary Redmond series, starts with demon trouble, and as of book seven, ends with demon trouble. There's going to be more books in that series, but the arc of the first seven books is done now, and there was a lot of demon stuff involved.

My spin off of that series doesn't even pretend. It's called the Demon Witch series, and follows the early years of one of Cary Redmond's best friends, the witch Angie Jordan. A character that shows up in both series is the legendary demon hunter, Aidan. Demon. Hunter. Legend. Of course, she also makes an appearance in this collection. She has a habit of showing up when demons are around. Just saying. There's also a second novella in this collection with a not-so-subtle nod to the Demon Witch series, as well. Hard to avoid when my theme matched so perfectly with those books.

The collection starts with *Friday's Curious Shop* (and yes that's spelled correctly), my ode to an old TV show from the late 80s that I dedicated many a Friday night's viewing to. The show, for the other Olds reading this, was *Friday the 13th the Series*—not related in any way to the Friday the 13th movies about Jason the relentless killer of teenage campers. I loved that TV show in all its creepy, spooky campiness. At the time, I loved being scared and watched a lot of spooky TV and movies—think *Creepshow, Elvira Mistress of the Dark, Tales from the Crypt*. This show stuck with me over the years, and while I'm not sure it would hit quite the same way now, in 2022, as it did back in the 80s, my memories of it are fond ones.

By the way, the spelling… I had meant to write Curios, not Curious, when I typed in the title for this story, but when I caught the spelling mistake, I loved it. Kept it. And it fits really well with the story. (My youngest loved the title too—no, he didn't read the story. This is grown up fantasy, and he is not a grown up yet. But he likes helping with things like titles.)

Given the inspiration for this one is a series, I might end up turning this story into a series as well. We'll see. Oh, and Cary Redmond readers, there's an easter egg in here. I'm curious (pun intended) if you'll spot it. I might have been too subtle. LOL

Next up, *Anger Management*. This is the novella featuring

the above-mentioned legendary demon hunter, Aidan. But it's not her story. It's actually the story of a dhampir with an anger issue. I wrote this novella at the same time as I was writing a light, low angst contemporary romance novel (Designed for You, if you're interested). I wrote both in the autumn of 2021, when I was feeling overwhelmed and scared sending my kids back to school in the midst of an ongoing pandemic—while my youngest still didn't have a vaccine—and angry with so much going on in the world at that time. I have a core of anger that got fed by all the turmoil of that year here in the US. And while the light contemporary romance helped me escape from some of that overwhelm and worry, my anger needed an outlet, too. That's where my dhampir Quinn came in. I actually had a dream one night in which I met this character for the first time. The next morning, I started her story. Couldn't help myself. I went back and forth between this novella and the romance novel. Two very different moods, but both helped me get through a tough time. And, despite the heavier and very angry mood of this novella, it was really fun to write.

Burning Inside a Stone Circle is the now-for-something-a-little-different story in the collection. The demons here are all internal, though the struggle to face them is still a matter of more than just personal destruction. The demons in this story are ones I related to strongly. And it might be too personal a story to release into the wide world. Only, I know everyone will bring their own experiences and perspective to it and won't view it quite the same way I do, so that helps. I won't say which parts are personal and which are made up, mainly because I want you to read the story, not spoil it in the introduction! I will say, though, I cried both while writing this one and during the edits. Frankly, that surprised me. By the edits, I'd forgotten how much of me I'd put into the story (and how much I'd held back). But what's that saying about writers? All we do is sit down in front of the blank page and open a vein? Well, in many ways, that's what I did in *Burning Inside a Stone Circle*. No regrets.

Next, we get back to actual demons. Or…*maybe* actual demons? That's the mystery of it all. And *The Museum of Small Art's Everyman* is more of mysterious story. A crime story, with a murder, inside a museum, surrounding by demonic art. There's not a lot I can say about it, though, without giving potential spoilers. So I will just say this is another one that I can see lending itself to series potential—I really liked the heroine, Anne, and her dynamic with the police detective. But that's all I'll say about it here. Mysteries are best left mysterious.

To finish up, we have *Demonic Dates*. This is the other story that links into the Demon Witch series in a peripheral way. The witch at the heart of this novella is mentioned in Spiderweb Witch, book two in the series. I'm the kind of writer who writes into the dark, without outlining, and so when I started this story, I thought I was writing a certain kind of tale. I was a little surprised by the turns it took, but pleasantly so. I hope readers enjoy those turns as much as I did.

This one also harkens more to my paranormal romance roots than anything else in the collection, because of course, I had to write at least one story like that. The theme of demons, and haunts and howls, is of course here again, but a secondary theme of anger seems to have worked its way into these stories, and is evident again in this final entry. I suppose that makes sense when dealing with stories about demons.

I ended with this particular novella because I really liked the way the last line of this story brings the entire collection to a close.

I hope readers enjoy these newest Haunts and Howls, in all their spooky fun. And if you're interested in the Demon Witch series after you've finished this book, just keep reading for an excerpt from Bone Lantern Witch, book one in the series.

Thanks for reading!

~Kat

FRIDAY'S CURIOUS SHOP

CHAPTER ONE

Riley checked the job listing on her phone. Again. Then looked at the storefront. Again. Yup. This was the place.

Friday's Curious Shop.

Not curios. No. Curious.

And to be fair, it was a pretty curious place.

But it wasn't just the spelling mistake—was it a mistake? —that gave her pause. The store itself didn't engender a lot of trust. Located off a side street in Queens near a massive train depot, lots of personal storage unit buildings, and a few truck parking lots, it wasn't exactly in a place that got a lot of foot traffic. She'd have assumed an antique-collectibles store would have to at least be in a place where people could find it and might go in spontaneously. It took *effort* to find this place. She'd walked around the area three times before she'd spotted the sign just off the weird triangle intersection, down a dead end side street that looked awkward banging up against the elevated tracks behind it.

If she went down another of the streets off the triangle intersection, the local fire department and a pharmacy sat next to each other looking perfectly ordinary. And a gas station with a little sundries shop sat at the front of the intersection along Northern Boulevard. The smell of days old trash and gasoline cut sharper in the bitter cold early winter air—another less than appealing lure for pedestrian traffic—and the sound of the N train rumbling past was almost loud enough to block out the sounds of honking traffic on road behind her.

Did she really want to do this interview? She needed a job something bad. Her part of the rent was due in a week and she was down to her last few dollars. If she had a job, with money actually coming in, she knew her roommates would float her this month's rent long enough for her to get her first paycheck. Without a job, though, they'd kick her out and get someone who could cover their bills. There was no sentimentality in the New York rental life.

Riley didn't have anywhere else to go. If they kicked her out, she'd be living on the street or bumming space on a friend's couch. Neither option appealed, especially with winter approaching fast.

Could she really afford to be picky about where she worked? If things didn't pan out, she could stay long enough to get a little cushion of money and find a new job. Then she could quit.

That was, if she even got the job.

She still had to do the interview. Which wasn't going to happen if she kept stalling, standing like an idiot on the sidewalk, looking between her phone and the storefront across the street.

Pulling in a deep breath, she checked for traffic—which seemed excessively cautious as this was a dead end street with nothing on it but Friday's Curious Shop. There was even street parking still free, and yet no one seemed to turn down the road to take advantage of it, even though parking in this area was at a premium this time of day. She considered that as she jogged across the street to the store.

Friday's Curious Shop had an elaborate wooden sign hanging out front, decorative and large with scrollwork around the name, which was written in some sort of calligraphy design and painted gold against a maroon background. It looked like something out of a different century.

Which in and of itself wouldn't have been bad. Riley liked old things, and sometimes felt a little out of touch with modern times—except where her cellphone was concerned; they'd have to pry that from her cold, dead hands to get it away from her—so the idea of working in a shop full of old things had appealed to her. She knew, since the store was in Queens and not Manhattan, that the antiques probably weren't the sort of thing sold at Christies, but she'd have bet a knowledgeable collector would find something valuable. She didn't really know. She'd never had enough extra money to be a collector of anything. Still, she imagined a used and antique store, even in Queens, might be fun.

But the charm of the place ended at the sign, at least on the outside.

The building was very industrial and functional. The glass windows looking into the store revealed a lot of old brown things piled haphazardly around the place, hard to even distinguish as individual items. There might have been an old wheel? And was that a rusted can? That half rag, half porcelain doll with a torn gray dress and no eyes wasn't creepy *at all*.

She shivered.

Did she really need the money this bad?

An icy breeze tunneled down the street, tugging at her

worn wool coat and the little bobble at the end of her knit cap, reminding her how very much she did not want to be homeless next month.

She gave the glass front door an experimental shove. It opened soundlessly and smoothly, a little jingle from an overhead bell the only thing announcing a new customer. She wasn't sure why she'd expected the door to screech in protest, like the hinges were rusted. Like no one had opened the front door in years. The place just sort of *felt* that way. Old, neglected, tossed aside.

For some reason, that made her sad.

The interior of the store hit her with dim light and hot air. Compared to the harshly bright winter light outside, that darkness forced her to a stop just inside the door while her eyes adjusted. The surrounding dust made her sneeze three times in rapid succession. Yeah, if she got the job, she was going to need to take antihistamines every day. She couldn't really afford antihistamines.

She blinked as her eyes finally adapted to the low lighting and she got her first good look at her surroundings. She stood perfectly still, afraid if she moved, she'd bump into something. Because there was a lot of stuff. A *lot* of stuff. Everywhere. Piled on tables, freestanding against walls, piled in the center of the floor. There seemed to be narrow paths cut through the detritus which wove through the store, but she couldn't see any other immediate organization. Dolls were piled with books next to a chipped tea pot by some tin boxes sitting on top of an old piano against which paintings in huge wooden frames were stacked. Some of the stuff looked like it might just be valuable—contradicting her earlier opinion of the place—but a person would have to be a determined picker to find the valuable in the midst of the chaos.

"Duck!"

The shout from somewhere in the middle of the stacks of stuff startled Riley so much she actually did duck while looking up. She expected one of the taller piles of stuff to be toppling over on top of her. Instead, she watched a very modern, small drone dip and sway overhead, before barreling past toward the back of the store.

"Sorry about that," said the same voice that had warned her to duck.

She stood slowly, hesitantly, and turned to face the voice. A man roughly the size of a bear stepped from between a stack of books and a large instrument case—maybe for a base fiddle or something? She wasn't sure. The man was dressed in tweed dress pants, a button-down white shirt, and a vest with a red tartan pattern on the front and black silk on the back. All of which stretched comfortably over a thick, but not fat, body. His red hair and beard were long and blended together so she couldn't really tell what was hair from his head and hair from his face, but the whole mass was neatly trimmed and clean. There was just a lot of hair. His features beyond all the hair were wide and strong. He had that ruddy color on his cheeks that a lot of white people with red hair seemed to get. His eyes were deep brown, and his brows heavy.

She had no idea how old the man was. With the full beard and mustache covering so much of his face, she had a hard time judging. There were faint creases around his eyes and between his eyebrows, but the furrows on his forehead seemed more from his frown than permanent signs of age.

"Damned thing goes the opposite direction it's supposed to," he grumbled.

It took her a minute to realize he was talking about the small drone.

"Not sure why Doreen thought it would be a good idea."

He tossed a remote-control hand unit onto the stack of books, and brushed his hands together as if dusting something from the remote off. "You here for the job?"

"Um. Yes. I'm Riley Anderson." She wasn't sure if she should offer her hand or not. She was so off balance by the drone skimming over her head and the sudden appearance of the large man, things like manners and proper interview behaviors went clean out of her head. She did remember to pull her hat off and stuff it into her coat pocket.

"Good to meet you, Riley Anderson." The man solved her to-handshake-or-not-to-handshake problem by reaching out with one large hand.

His fingers engulfed hers completely, but his firm, quick handshake was very gentle. Obviously, he was used to being twice the size of everyone else around him.

"This way. Doreen will want to meet you."

She stumbled after him through the narrow path between walls of stuff—how the hell did he get through this store without knocking things over?—and cleared her throat. "I…I didn't get your name?"

"Oh." He stopped abruptly and faced her. "Sorry. Ian Sinclair. Doreen is my sister. We own this place."

"Who's Friday?"

A smile broke through the beard and mustache. "That was our great-grandmother's name."

"Friday Sinclair?"

"Don't ask."

He led her deeper into the store, until eventually they reached a cluttered wooden counter near a back wall that was covered in shelves piled with even more stuff. At least, she assumed that wall was the back wall. She'd gotten turned around in all the stacks and wasn't entirely sure which direction the front door was anymore. She'd need a map to navigate this place.

It seemed larger inside than it had looked from the outside, too. With all the clutter, she'd assumed it would feel small. It certainly felt claustrophobic. But the trek from the area near the front door to this wooden counter had taken…time.

She frowned and glanced behind her, but blinked back to her surroundings when Ian introduced the woman sitting behind the counter.

"This is Doreen. She handle's the books and keeps track of inventory. I'm customer care and acquisitions."

"We're both acquisitions," the woman said, her brow raised and her mouth pinched as she looked at her brother.

"Fair enough," he said with a sigh. "Both acquisitions. She is better with the books, though."

"True enough." She turned a smile on Riley that was both polite and pointed. "You're here for the job?"

"Yes," Riley stuttered. "Uh… Yes." She was fumbling this, badly, but the whole place left her off center and a little confused. She wasn't even sure why. Maybe the sheer amount of stuff everywhere was just disorienting. "I'm Riley, by the way. Riley Anderson."

"Good to meet you," Doreen said. "Welcome to Friday's."

She was a red-head like her brother, and her hair was just as curly, but she had it pulled back into a low ponytail that kept it away from her face. She was pretty, pale, freckled, and also of an indeterminant age. Her dress sense was a little less dramatic than her brother's—no tweed and tartan mixes. Just a simple emerald green turtleneck and a purple and black striped skirt over thick-soled, chunky boots. Her glasses looked heavy duty, thick plastic brown frames that suited her face, but lenses that seemed weighty.

Riley's own glasses felt a little less substantial in comparison. Not that she had them on right now—they were old and she needed an updated prescription since she didn't see out of them as well as she did her contacts. So she wore the contacts she'd been nursing along for the last year. She needed new ones of those, too. But she needed a job with health insurance first. Mostly the job part. If she could manage her allergies in this place, she was prepared to start tomorrow.

Except the siblings had barely said anything. Interview. Get through the interview without fucking up first.

Doreen said, "What about the ad attracted your attention?"

She held Riley's gaze as she asked, the stare seemingly casual, but Riley felt the look as if Doreen was peering through her soul.

Riley shook off the uncomfortable feeling to say, "I like old things, and dealing with people who like old things. I always have."

"Spent a lot of time in antique and curio stores?"

"Thrift shops mostly," Riley admitted, hoping the state of her thrift shop coat and slacks helped her case here and didn't detract from her suitability for the job.

"That all?" Doreen asked.

Riley shrugged and decided they looked like people who would appreciate honesty. "And you actually listed the starting salary, so I knew what I was getting into." She glanced around, frowning a little. A shop like this being able to pay a decent starting wage was…unexpected. But she wasn't going to look a gift horse in the mouth. For all she knew, the siblings were rich and this was their side business, and they had plenty of money to pour into it. "Not everyone wants to tell what they're paying upfront."

"Told you," Ian said.

He hadn't gone behind the counter to join his sister, but was instead standing a few feet from Riley with his thick arms crossed over his massive chest, looking like a giant bear trying to look like a less giant, more harmless bear.

Riley appreciated the effort.

"Anything else in the advert that caught your attention?" Doreen asked, ignoring her brother.

Riley thought back to the listing on the job-finder app. She couldn't really place anything in particular. She liked that they listed salary. The added bonus of benefits included was also nice. And after all the time she'd spent in thrift shops over the years, she figured she'd be able to handle a curios shop. She had assumed the "curious" part of the store's name in the ad had been a misspelling, but obviously it wasn't. Which made her—ironically?—curious about how the store got that name.

"Mostly, I just thought I'd be able to do the job," Riley answered after a moment of enduring Doreen's stare. She almost said the "no experience necessary" part had been another big draw but was a little afraid that was a step too far in the honesty department. She needed this job really badly. That meant coming across like she *wanted* to work here, in a place like this.

To be fair, it couldn't possibly be worse than her last two jobs.

Doreen exchanged a look with her brother that Riley was sure had more meaning than was obvious to an outsider. She stuffed her hands in her coat pockets so she wouldn't visibly fidget, but her fingers were doing a twisting dance in her pockets as she tried to calm her racing pulse. Despite the heat in the place, she felt a little clammy and cold under the threadbare wool and decided keeping the coat on was a good idea.

Doreen opened her mouth, as if to say something else, then snapped it shut. And glared at the front door moments before the bell sounded to announce a new customer.

The fact that someone had walked in off the street surprised Riley, but maybe the place had a following, people going out of their way to visit the store. Maybe it wouldn't be a boring job of mostly dusting and rearranging old junk. Not that she'd object to boring and dusting and rearranging, so long as it paid on time.

Ian grunted something under his breath, gave his sister another look, then walked toward the front of the store.

Quietly enough Riley wasn't sure she was supposed to hear her, Doreen said, "Hadn't intended a diving-into-the-deep end test."

Riley glanced between Doreen and the general direction of the front door—easier to pinpoint now that she'd heard the bell. Although, given the quantity of stuff and the labyrinth of piles that had to be navigated, it was also possible sound was distorted and she still didn't really know where the front of the building was.

She was actually considering asking Doreen when a noise from somewhere off in the piles stopped her. Sounded almost like a growl. Then a shout…

And then something crashed to the floor in a cascade of clattering metal and wood.

*R*iley startled back closer to the wooden counter, away from the sound of curios toppling. She glanced between the noise and Doreen, who hadn't risen from her seat behind the counter yet.

"Is everything okay? Should…should we help Ian?"

Doreen gave her a sideways look but didn't say anything.

There was more noise from the front of the store, another crash, and then someone yelled, "I need it back! Don't you understand. I *need* it!"

More crashing. Ian shouted, "Get back here."

And Doreen cursed under her breath. "Here, take this."

She pulled something out from under the counter, and for a moment, Riley thought Doreen was handing her a gun, which would have been pointless since Riley didn't have the first clue how to handle a gun and hated the things anyway. But what Doreen handed her was a small leather satchel, like the kind of thing that might hold dice or marbles or other small toys.

"Hold this," Doreen said, her gaze on the shouts and crashes coming from somewhere in the depths of the store.

"And do exactly what I say. Don't question it. There's not time. Do you understand?"

"Not even a little bit." But she stuffed the satchel into her coat pocket and waited for Doreen to tell her what to do next.

Doreen finally stood from the three-legged bar stool she'd been sitting on and came around to the front of the counter. She pulled something out from under her turtleneck shirt, a pendant hanging from a long silver chain. In her other hand she was holding something that looked a little like a small, silver dagger that poked through the bottom of a delicate, etched silver bowl.

Riley wanted to ask questions, but the noise and shouts were getting louder, and Doreen had told her not to ask questions anyway. This was not like any other job interview she'd ever been on.

A second later, more crashes and then someone—something?—came barreling through the store's clutter, knocking things over in its wake. The…person or whatever was shouting, and from somewhere behind it, Riley heard Ian shouting, too. A lot of, "Get back here, you bastard," from Ian and, "Give it to me!" from the…person.

She wasn't sure what about the person had her hesitating to call them a person. Probably the glowing red eyes. Maybe it was the way they loped almost on all fours. Might have been the sharp spikes sticking out of their back through their clothes—clothes that were in worse shape than most her worn wardrobe, which was really saying something. The…person's clothes weren't much better than rags, but the rags covered all the important bits. Left the sharp, black, shiny spikes sticking out, though. And some of the exposed arm and leg parts. Which were covered in green scales.

The green scales really threw her.

What the hell kind of cosplay was this?

The…person looked up, spotted Doreen, and charged right for her. Whatever the person was, they were big. Bigger than they'd looked loping through the shop bent over and using all four limbs. When they stood up, their head nearly brushed the ceiling.

"I can't stay like this," the person shouted. "I need it back!"

"It was never yours to begin with," Doreen said, her voice a lot calmer than Riley was feeling in that moment. "You shouldn't have had it."

"It was mine!"

The…person took a swipe at Doreen, Doreen hit them with the knife-like thing she was carrying—not stabbed, she *hit* the person with it, using the side of the blade and pushing it into the person's arm.

"Missed," Doreen hissed under her breath. To Riley, she said, "Get ready."

Riley had no idea what she was supposed to be getting ready. The bag in her pocket she assumed. She pulled it out and held it, but…what was she going to do with it? Use the whole thing? Or was she supposed to take something out of it? Doreen had said no questions, so she kept her mouth shut. But she had questions.

Lots and lots of questions.

The green-scaled person rose up to their full height, giving Riley a good view of their arm where Doreen had pressed the dagger-like thing…and the smoking black patch of scaly skin where the knife had touched them. The person slapped a hand at the smoking patch, their eyes flared brighter red, and then they dropped to all fours, their shoulders seeming to move around on their back so that the position looked a lot more natural than it should from something vaguely human-shaped just moments ago.

"I need it back," the person roared again. "I can't stop this without it." And they charged Doreen again, head down, spikes along the back up.

"Now!" Doreen shouted.

Without having the first clue what Doreen meant, Riley opened the bag and tossed its contents at the rapidly approaching…person.

What flew out of the bag was not exactly what Riley had been expecting, but then again, she hadn't had a clue what to expect.

So she wasn't sure why she was surprised by green slime.

The bag hadn't felt like it was holding liquid. It had felt like there were marbles in it or rocks. But what came out was a stream of thick, viscous, goopy green liquid. Sort of liquid. A little thick to really be called liquid. Definitely more like slime.

The slime slapped against the charging creature, along their burnt arm and the side of their face.

Then the creature was on top of Doreen, shoving Riley aside so hard she slammed up against a table piled with stuff and went crashing to the ground along with whatever stuff had been on the table.

Doreen shouted, screamed. There was a lot of screaming. By the time Riley pulled herself out from under the tangle of stuff, Ian had jumped into the fray and was trying to wrap his arm around the person's neck while not simultaneous getting stabbed by the back spines. Doreen was under the creature, pushing up with her knife-thing pressed right into the creature's chest.

There was smoke, and the stench of burning… Well, it was worse than burning flesh. It smelled like something putrid was roasted, releasing noxious fumes that made her gag and very nearly throw up.

She held that impulse in as she clambered to her feet, trying not to breath too deeply.

Ian shouted something to Doreen, Doreen cursed up a storm and pressing the knife-thing against the green-scaled person again and again. The slime Riley had thrown against the creature was soaking *into* their scales but otherwise Riley couldn't see what it was doing.

Couldn't miss the person's hands reaching for Doreen's neck, though.

Those hands weren't like a normal human's. Fingers too long and bony, tipped by black claws instead of nails. But Riley's adrenaline and fear were so high, she barely noticed. She charged forward and grabbed hold of a thick scaly wrist, holding one hand away from Doreen.

The person was strong as hell and struggled against her, swinging out their arm in a way that would have sent Riley careening into the table again if she hadn't held on so tightly. The creature wiggled their arm again, trying to throw Riley off, lifting her almost off the ground.

She kept her toes in contact with the scuffed wooden floor, if barely, and it was enough to keep her from being rag-dolled around.

Getting rag-dolled into the person's back spikes struck her as a bad idea.

She heaved downward, putting all her weight into keeping her feet on the ground and her hold on the scale-covered wrist. The person reached for Doreen again, dragging at Riley's grip. The scales made the creature slippery, slick, hard to hold. She wrapped both hands around the wrist, clenching tight, and pulled hard.

"Stop messing around," Ian shouted. "Do it!"

"Can't," Doreen shouted back, then cursed some more as she shoved the knife-thing against the person's forehead.

They roared and threw themselves upward, which brought Riley up to her toes again and flung Ian off into a stack of magazines and tin boxes.

Doreen used the moment's freedom from the creature's weight to scramble up to her knees. She gripped the pendant hanging around her neck and started chanting.

Still holding onto the creature—impossible to think of someone covered in scales and spikes with glowing red eyes as anything but a creature—Riley desperately tried to keep it from lunging at Doreen again.

She felt like her arms were going to be pulled from the sockets, though. The creature was strong! And without Ian on the other side, the creature dragged Riley forward as they tried to reach Doreen again, dragging Rikey along the floor as she attempted to pull them backward.

Riley had no idea what Doreen was saying, she wasn't speaking—chanting?—in English. But whatever it was sounded nonsensical. Not like a real language even. Sounds shaped like words without meaning.

Whatever she was saying, though, had an effect on the creature. They screeched, a sound so loud Riley cringed and wanted to cover her ears. But that would mean letting go of the creature and they were still reaching for Doreen.

Slower now, though, Riley realized.

Ian scrambled back to his feet and grabbed the creature's other arm just as they swiped vicious claws at Doreen. Doreen didn't move, or try to duck away, which Riley found both brave and stupid.

The creature screeched again, a sound no human should make. "No! No! It's not fair. It's not fair!"

In the back of her mind, Riley thought, what the hell is fair? Why would you think life was fair? If life was fair, she'd be able to pay rent this month and not be worried about ending up on the street. If life was fair, she'd be able to afford an apartment to herself or with just one roommate, not three roommates in a tiny one bedroom. If life was fair, she'd have more than a few bucks in her bank account—money that was going to get sucked away by fees for not having enough money in the account.

Life wasn't fair. Life often wasn't even kind. But you took what it gave you and made the best of it. And sometimes there was luck. Riley didn't think life was required to be fair, but she did believe in luck.

She believed in bad luck a lot. But she also believed in good luck. It was just sometimes hard to tell which was which.

All this went through her mind in the split second before the creature gave a mighty tug that nearly pulled her off her feet again. She stumbled forward, clenching desperately at the scaly, slippery wrist while simultaneously trying to avoid the spine spikes that kept swinging in her direction as the creature thrashed.

Doreen reached up with her pendant in one hand and her knife-thing in the other as the creature hovered over her, with only Ian and Riley's efforts holding sharp claws back from Doreen's throat.

Then Ian shouted, "Let go. Now!"

Horrified, terrified, she nearly asked a question. Nearly protested. But Doreen had told her not to, and to do what was said instantly, so she let go of the creature despite everything in her telling her the creature would kill Doreen if she did.

She stepped away quickly to avoid another slash of back spikes, bumped up against a table and sent piles of playing cards crashing to the ground. Half sprawled against the table for balance, she looked up in time to see Doreen press the knife-thing against the creature's chest again and the pendant against its forehead.

The creature screamed.

And the slime that had soaked into the scaley skin started to seep back out again, like a thick, green sweat.

The stuff poured from the creature. But it didn't fall onto the floor or Doreen. It moved over the creature's body toward the pendant, moved like it was drawn to the pendant. A magnet pulling in a mass of tiny metal filings. The slime swarmed over every part of the creature, obscuring them, encasing them, even as it flowed toward the pendant.

Into the pendant.

There was a lot more slime coming out than there had been going in. The pendant wasn't a large piece, maybe two, two and half inches in diameter, a flat disk of metal. Nothing in it that should have held that much slime.

Yet still, the viscous green liquid flowed into the pendant as if there was room, as if the flat disk was actually a deep vase that could hold all that slime without trouble.

The moments the process took felt like several hours. But finally, the slime seemed to stop flowing out of the creature. It thinned as it disappeared into the pendant, slowly revealing non-scaled human legs. Then a non-scaled human torso without back spikes. And finally, a human head covered in wet brown hair.

The person flopped limply to one side, helped by the quick reflexes of Ian to land gently on the wooden floor beside Doreen. She rolled away from the person and slowly got to her feet, holding the pendant carefully away from her body.

"Well. That was a bit of fun," Ian said.

CHAPTER THREE

*D*oreen snorted, her only response to her brother's comment. She closed her eyes, let out a long breath, and when she opened her eyes again, she was looking directly at Riley.

Riley, who wasn't sure whether to start screaming, or run for the front door—if she could even find it—or start cleaning up the overturned table behind her. She blinked in the dim store, trying not to sneeze from the dust they'd kicked up during the fight, looking between the fallen person, who looked like a person now, and the pendant Doreen was holding so carefully.

"Help me put this away," Doreen said, lifting the pendant a little, but without explaining anything at all. "Ian will take care of our unhappy customer."

That was a customer? What had they bought?

What the hell was going on?

Riley glanced back at the person on the floor and Ian as she followed Doreen behind the counter. The person—she could see they were probably a man now—still had on the ragged clothes he'd worn when he'd been covered in scales, so he wasn't dressed for being outside on a day this cold. In fact, his pale white skin looked nearly blue now that it wasn't covered in scales. But since he seemed unconscious, and it didn't look like Ian was going to heft him out the door in that state, she figured he'd be okay. At least, she hoped so. Plus, she was pretty sure she'd seen some piles of folded clothing somewhere in all the mess of stuff filling the store. There had to be a pair of pants and a t-shirt in there somewhere.

She turned back to Doreen as Doreen pressed a button under the wooden counter and a door in the back wall that Riley hadn't even seen opened with a slight groan and a hiss of escaping air. The escaping air sounded suspiciously like a word, but a word in a language Riley didn't know.

Weird.

For a split second, she hesitated to walk through that doorway. But curiosity got the better of her. And she really needed a job. Even a weird one. So long as the paycheck didn't bounce. She was still conscious of wanting to make a good impression on her potential employers, despite the fact that what had just happened was completely crazy and maybe working in a place like this wouldn't be good for her survival prospects.

The instinct to run screamed through the back of her mind —what had just happened couldn't be real, and she needed to get out of here, and this was all nuts—while at the same time visions of her dire financial situation rushed in and encircled the desire to escape the store. This was the only place that had gotten back to her after she'd sent out dozens and dozens of applications. And as her grandmother had always said, "Beggars couldn't be choosers."

So she followed Doreen through the doorway, hesitant but curious enough to get around her reluctance. She told the "run, run, run!" scream in her mind to quiet down. They didn't have time to run screaming from a job that paid this much an hour.

The room beyond the doorway was significantly darker than the main part of the store. And if possible smelled dustier. Riley sneezed again.

"Sorry about the dust," Doreen said. "This much stuff in one place has a tendency to collect dust no matter what we do."

"No problem," Riley said, surprised her voice came out normal. Surprised they were having such a mundane conversation after what had just happened.

Whatever the hell it was that had just happened.

The dark room held the sort of musty, overstuffed smell of a storage room, but it felt a lot bigger and more open beyond the darkness than the main shop. And there was another smell under the dust Riley couldn't quite place. Bit like ozone burning, like after a lightning strike. Maybe. Hard to tell because she was trying not to breath in the dust too deeply and start another sneezing fit. But musty, stuffy, and lightning were a weird enough combination that she didn't notice Doreen moving away from her at first.

She scrambled forward, wanting to catch up and not get lost in the dark, but before she'd taken two steps a voice floated back through the blackness ahead.

"Don't move yet," Doreen said. "I need to get the light and don't want you to trip."

Riley froze. Probably an insurance worry. Couldn't blame Doreen for that. Insurance was a bitch. One of the banes of Riley's existence—well a bane because she didn't have any and that limited her options with things like, oh, new glasses and contact lenses. And medical emergencies if she tripped and hurt herself at a place where she was applying for a job.

Overhead lights flickered on a moment later, bright and

strong enough after the darkness to rob her of vision for a few moments. She squinted against the glare, waiting for her eyes to adjust. When they finally did, she remained frozen in place, afraid to move any farther into the room.

She was surrounded by shelves, which seemed to stretch out much farther in front of her than the building should have allowed—were there mirrors lining the back wall?—and each shelf contained piles and stacks and boxes full of… Well, she wasn't entirely sure what.

There were bottles of liquid that glowed, sharp edged weapons, and something that looked like a shield sticking out of one box. Books that fluttered in a breeze that didn't exist. To her left, a strange looking crow stared down at her from a high shelf, and it took her several moments to ensure it wasn't a real crow, just stuffed.

There were things that looked like pendants, like the one Doreen wore, except they were all different—different shapes, designs, thicknesses, colors, materials—and some where haphazardly thrown together while others were placed in their own little pocket of space with nothing else around them. Given how packed the shelves where, those lone amulets without close contact with anything else made her shudder for primal reasons she couldn't explain.

Beyond the amulets, pendants, bottles, books, weapons, and jars full of things she couldn't identify, there were also clear boxes filled with…ordinary things like porcelain and plastic dolls, tin boxes, scarves, t-shirts, glasses, crystal goblets, dinnerware, small toys, and board games. All the kind of stuff she expected in a second-hand store, expected to see on the tables and shelves outside. She might have just thought they were extra stock. Except that the clear boxes they were in weren't plastic, they were made of glass. And the lids covering them were sealed with a lock-like bracket covered in glowing symbols. She wanted to call them runes except she didn't know what runes were supposed to look like.

There wasn't a single thing on any of the shelves immediately surrounding her that looked…safe.

A shiver crawled along her spine.

To make matters worse, the place didn't just smell funny. It *sounded* strange. Whispers, just beyond her hearing. Shuffling and shifting, like things were settling. Scrambling, against glass, against metal and wood. The New Yorker in her immediately wanted to look for evidence of mice—and then race to the nearest subway and never return. She had had to live in a few apartments over the years with uncontrolled mice problems. She was phobic about them now, and some of those high-pitched scritching noises were bringing back seriously bad memories.

"You have mice in here?" she called to Doreen who was hidden among the shelves still.

"Not mice," Doreen said. "Well, not living mice anyway."

Ew. That nearly drove Riley back out of the storage room. Nearly. Only the thought of having to live in the subway tunnels to keep from freezing to death, and being surrounded by subway rats—significantly bigger and less scared of humans than apartment mice—kept her in place. But it was a close thing.

The whispering seemed to ebb and flow, like a tide, coming into hearing range and then out again. All the fluttering and shifting sounds made her skin crawl. She tried to tell herself it was just Doreen moving things around. Except Doreen's voice had come from somewhere off to the right, and not all the sounds were coming from that direction.

Something to her left laughed. A high, piercing, chittering sort of laugh that ended on a sob.

Riley clenched her teeth together to keep from screaming. That was probably just one of the dolls, right? Or another toy. Something with its battery dying so it made noise suddenly. Without being handled or touched.

Her Gran had had this doll from when she was a kid, a teddy bear with a little box inside that, if you pressed in the right spot, played Christmas songs. When the batteries were dying on the bear, it would spontaneously burst into song even when no one was nearby. She was going to just assume that's where that eerie laugh was coming from, a toy with its battery dying, and not question why someone would own a toy that made that monumentally creepy laugh in the first place. Maybe that was why the toy was here. Because no one *wanted* to own it.

"Uhm," Riley called, wanting to get out of this place pretty badly, but also not wanting to sacrifice any hope she had of getting this job—did she still want the job? She needed it desperately, so yes, she did. "Do you need help?"

"Walk straight ahead—do *not* go down any other aisle than the one you're facing—and then turn right when you reach the back of the room," Doreen said. "Do not touch anything either."

Riley's hands trembled as she started down the narrow corridor made by the bracketing shelves. She carefully didn't touch anything, trying to suck in her shoulders and hips so she'd be narrower and not risk brushing against anything. Something with paper fluttered on a shelf near her head, and she stepped away so fast, she nearly bumped the shelf behind her. Something on that shelf made a sound like a whisper of words Riley couldn't understand.

She jumped back to the center of the aisle, nearly panting. Forcing herself to take a deep breath, she continued toward the rear of the storage room, which felt very far away.

She was nearly to the back of the row of shelves—a journey that felt like it had taken ages, but she knew objectively only lasted a few moments—when she heard someone whisper her name.

"Riley."

Quiet. Almost too quiet to hear, but distinct enough she knew it was her name. She frowned. Was that Doreen? She glanced around. Maybe Doreen was closer than she'd thought. Or maybe Ian had followed them back to the storage room?

But no. No sign of either of the store owners. Just lots of stuff on shelves. Lots of stuff Riley didn't want to touch.

A dagger caught her attention. And despite herself, she edged closer to the shelf to get a better look at it. Maybe a foot long, including the handle. The handle—what was that called again?—was wrapped in black leather with a twist of silver thread-like metal encircling it. The top of the handle—pommel, maybe?—had a little round hunk of smooth silver on it and there was a very small hand guard near the blade, forming a t-shape. The blade was smooth and silver, though there seemed to be little flashes of blue running over the surface. Probably from some light reflection? Riley looked around but couldn't spot the source of the blue light.

"Riley."

She gasped and looked back at the dagger.

A dagger couldn't talk. She was hearing things. She had to be hearing things.

She reached for the handle—pommel, whatever—curious to feel the silver threaded against the leather. A stab of jealousy hit her, that there were people in the world who could afford something like this, something purely for decorative purposes, while she couldn't make rent. Hardly seemed fair. Not right, some had so much while she had so little.

She stopped herself from touching the dagger at the last minute, her finger hovering over the blade. Doreen had said not to touch anything. This was something. She flashed on the person…man who'd torn through the front of the shop, with his scales and spine spikes. Looking for something from here…

Fisting her hand, she stepped back from the blade. Yeah, maybe touching stuff in here was a bad idea. Just in case.

She turned away from the dagger, though for some reason it took an effort. There was a tugging on her brain almost, like she should really turn around and touch the dagger. That was something she *needed* to do.

But no. What she needed was to make some money. And the person interviewing her for a decent paying job had told her not to touch anything. Probably a test of some sort. Maybe a hidden Bluetooth speaker near the dagger. Someone, possibly even Doreen, whispering her name. There was a lot of things in here likely to be valuable, if dusty. The Sinclairs wouldn't want to hire someone who might pocket some of the merchandise.

She firmed her spine and walked away from the dagger. She wasn't sure how a Bluetooth speaker might also cause her this strange compulsion to return to the thing and pick it up, but that was probably her own curiosity.

Her self-preservation instincts and need for a paying gig were a lot stronger than her curiosity, though. Desperation had a way of doing that for her.

When she reached the end of the aisle, the strange compulsion to return to the dagger eased.

Doreen appeared from the next aisle. She glanced behind Riley, frowning a little, but then just said, "This way."

CHAPTER FOUR

iley followed Doreen dutifully. She wanted to ask questions. She had a lot. But she also didn't want to say something that would fuck all this up, so she kept her mouth shut.

Doreen walked her along what Riley thought was the storage room's back wall. There weren't any mirrors back here to explain why it had looked like the shelves went on for miles. And when she glanced down another aisle as they passed, the way back now seemed very far away. Hadn't felt *that* long getting to this side of the room. So weird.

The number of rows of shelves seemed enormous, too. And yet they reached their destination in only a few moments. A metal shelving unit secured on the back wall that still had some space on it. In fact, there were several empty shelves. Given how packed the rest of the storage room was meant any space at all struck her as interesting. A quick glance around confirmed the shelves nearby were all stuffed full. She blinked as she turned back to the half empty unit.

And caught a flash of blue running along the unit's silver metal.

She blinked. Had to be some weird trick of the light back here. It wasn't bright light. Bright enough to see by and see clearly. But not a florescent bulb glare. And to her, the light had more of a yellow glow, making things look more sepia toned. Weirdly old fashioned actually. But none of it should have caused the blue flashes on silver metal.

A chittering sound startled her into moving a little closer to Doreen.

"Not mice, I promise," Doreen said, without looking at her. Under her breath, "Mice wouldn't dare come in here. Little bastards are too smart for that."

Uhm. That…didn't sound encouraging. Or even settling for her worry about things skittering across the floor. Now she was just worried about things that weren't mice—and she couldn't hardly imagine what those things might be. She didn't want to know.

"Do me a favor," Doreen said, without looking away from the shelf. "Hand me one of those glass containers."

She pointed to the side of the shelf, and sure enough there was a stack of glass jars, like short, squat Mason jars. Except the lids weren't metal. They were glass, attached to the jars by a thick, circular wire and with a metal clip to hold the lid down in an airtight seal. There was something etched into the surface of the lid, clear lines in the clear glass. A design Riley had never seen before but looked vaguely like scrolling curlicues over a circular shape with a triangle in the center.

Wait, she had seen that symbol before. A vague memory surfaced as she lifted one of the glass jars to hand to Doreen. That particular symbol. Somewhere… She couldn't place it. The memory remained vague.

Before she could look any closer at the symbol, though, Doreen took the jar and gently flipped the lid open with one hand, letting it hang back against the jar as she very gently placed her necklace with the round pendant inside. She held the necklace by the chain, Riley noticed, still not touching the pendant even as she slowly lowered it into the center of the glass jar. When the pendant was safely laying flat at the bottom of the jar, Doreen circled it with the chain, so that the chain also laid flat on the bottom, surrounding the pendant in a spiral of silver links.

Doreen's shoulders relaxed as she closed the lid and flipped the metal clasp closed. A clink clink sound when the clasp clicked into place, followed by a soft sighing exhale from the jar. The clear symbol on the top briefly flashed with a reddish color, so briefly Riley could almost believe she'd imagined it. Doreen gently set the jar onto the empty shelf at hip level, all the way to the left, as if it started a new row of stuff.

When she faced Riley again, her cheeks were flushed, her freckles standing out sharply against her white skin, and sweat dripped down her temples. It wasn't that hot in the storage room. In fact, if anything, Riley thought it felt a little chilly back here.

"So," Doreen said, swiping a hand over her curly hair, smoothing it back into the ponytail, "there will be a two-week trial period. You'll of course be paid the full hourly wage in that time. We'll need you to be here from eleven in the morning until seven at night most days. Some will days will be two in the afternoon until ten at night. Will those hours work for you?"

Riley nodded rapidly. But wait… What was happening?

"Good. Benefits won't start until we're all sure this job is the right fit. If you make it through the first two weeks, benefits kick in. Those include three weeks paid leave each year. Medical leave is negotiable and…dependent on circumstances."

The way she said that made Riley's stomach do a little nervous flip, though she wasn't entirely sure why.

But the nervousness paled in comparison to her relief as what Doreen was saying sunk in. "I got the job?" They hadn't really asked her any questions about her relevant experience or…really anything at all except for why their ad had drawn her interest. Maybe the whole scaled-person-attack thing had been a test of some kind?

What kind of test and what did it imply about this job, though?

"We'll also need you to sign a confidentiality agreement," Doreen continued as she started back the direction they'd come, walking briskly past the rows of shelves. She ignored Riley's question about whether or not she had the job.

Riley couldn't blame her since it was obvious she was telling her she had it—at least for a trial period.

Before following Doreen, she glanced back at the glass jar. And gasped.

The symbol on the top had changed. There was now an eye etched into the middle of the triangle. She was certain that hadn't been there before. The eye was just a basic outline, with a small circle in the center representing the iris. But at the very center of the iris, there seemed to be a little red dot.

She looked around. Where was that coming from?

And how the hell had she missed the eye in the center of the triangle the first time she'd looked at the symbol on the lid?

"Don't fall behind," Doreen called.

Riley looked up and realized Doreen was halfway back to where they'd started. She scrambled to catch up.

"Don't want to come back here on your own," Doreen said, continuing in the same no-nonsense tone as she'd used to outline the benefits and time off. "Too easy to get lost until you know your way around."

Riley frowned and glanced at all the neat rows of shelves. The place was huge, sure, a lot larger than she would have guessed from the outside of the building, but everything was in rows. How could she get lost back here? She'd just need to go to the front of the room and walk straight until she reached the door.

She didn't argue with Doreen, though. She had a trial at this job, and she'd be getting two weeks of pay even if she didn't make it through the trial period. That would be enough to placate her roommates and ensure she didn't end up homeless. At least not yet.

The journey back to the correct aisle seemed to take less time than it had taken to reach the shelf where they'd put the pendant. Doreen turned suddenly down a row that, as far as Riley could tell, looked a lot like any other row. As she followed Doreen, sticking close, she watched out for the dagger that had drawn her attention when she'd passed this way last time.

But she didn't see the dagger. In fact, everything looked a little different. There were still stacks of boxes and jars and weird things piled onto the shelves, but it all looked like different boxes and jars and weird things. And the fact that the dagger wasn't where she'd last seen it was pretty obvious.

They must be in a different row. Of course they were. Obviously. They'd turned too soon to have been in the same aisle. She was being silly. She rolled her eyes at herself. No wonder Doreen had warned her not to come back here alone.

When they emerged at the front of the storage room, she expected to walk a bit along the front wall before reaching the door back into the main store. If they'd turned earlier going this direction, they'd no longer be lined up with that door.

Except, they were. The door back into the store remained open just in front of them as they walked out of the aisle. Doreen walked through without hesitation, as if she'd expected it to be right there.

So either the aisle they'd been in had changed itself around drastically from when Riley had first walked down it. The shelves moved. Or the door back into the store moved.

None of which was possible.

She thought of the man with green scales and back spikes attacking Doreen. The way he'd returned to a more human form once that stuff had drained out of him and into Doreen's pendant. The pendant they'd just stored in a glass jar that now had an eye with a glowing red dot in the center of it etched into the lid. An eye that hadn't been there before.

Was the paycheck really worth…facing the reality of what she'd seen here today?

She was working hard not to acknowledge the strangeness. The spookiness. The fact that none of this stuff *should be happening*. She was working hard to pretend there were explanations. That logic applied. And that none of this was as weird as it seemed. Just seemed weird because she was new. She was desperate for the job. Desperate for the income—even a temporary job would buy her time and keep her off the streets for a few more weeks.

She could keep looking for another job while working here. That had been her intent all along. She didn't want to be a retail shop clerk for the rest of her life. That wasn't why she'd gone to college and racked up all those student loan debts she couldn't pay back. But she didn't have a fall back, any sort of backup if this fell through. No family to move in with. Very few friends who could take her in—they were all stretched to the limits too and didn't have the room or resources. She might find a few nights on someone's couch here or there, but those would only be short term options, a day or two at most.

She still had her winter coat on, she'd never had a chance to take it off before the interview got started, and sweat dripped in a line down her spine, sticky and uncomfortable under her button-down shirt. As they passed back into the main store, a whisper against Riley's ear had her glancing back quickly into the storage room.

Nothing was there. The shadows were still. And no air currents brushed her hair or cooled her sweat. Just a storage room. Just a room.

Just a job.

She only sneezed once when they stepped around the counter, and mentally put allergy pills on her "things to scam from roommates" list until she could afford to buy a bottle for herself. Lauren had bad allergies. She'd have something Riley could borrow.

The lights in the main store seemed brighter now, as if the winter sunlight penetrated the front windows and reached farther into the store now. And she realized as she glanced around, that was probably true. The mess created earlier was still a mess—tables overturned, a scarf box had toppled into a heap of colorful destruction, the tin boxes and old dolls and books lay in chaotic piles, some of the larger merchandise looked broken.

Doreen looked at the mess and sighed. Ian walked back to them from the front of the shop.

"Everything settled?" he asked, his gaze moving between Doreen and the now closed door to the storage room.

"Settled and settled." She faced Riley. "So. Are you ready to start work? If you don't have any other appointments this afternoon, maybe you could start your trial today?" She gestured at the mess and her mouth curved up in a wry smile. "We could use help cleaning this up."

Ian narrowed his gaze at Riley, assessing. She wasn't sure how he felt about the fact that his sister had summarily given her a trial shot at the job. Doreen hadn't even discussed that with him. But he wasn't arguing or asking to speak to Doreen alone. Maybe he approved the hire, too?

Riley hoped so. Because, "I don't have anything else this afternoon. I can definitely start now."

The sooner she started, the sooner she'd have her first pay check. The sooner she could stave off the inevitability of living on the streets.

A slight breeze whispered through the store, brushing the back of her neck. Cold. So not the heaters. Cold enough she wanted to shiver again, but she didn't dare. Both Doreen and Ian were staring at her, as if waiting for her to do…something.

She glanced around. "Is there a place I can hang my coat? Then I'll get to work cleaning things up."

Another look between the siblings. Then Doreen said, "You can put your coat behind the counter for now. We'll have a place ready for you tomorrow where you can store your personal things. We have a little break room through there."

She gestured to one side of the main floor, but Riley didn't see any doors. All she saw was more stuff.

"I'll have the official paperwork ready by tomorrow, too," Doreen said.

"Usually pretty quiet in here on a Tuesday," Ian said. "You'll have time to read through everything before signing."

"Sounds great." Riley tried to sound cheerful. Another of those cold breezes kissed the back of her neck.

And then she felt a strange sort of…opening. It was the

weirdest sensation. Like something that had been closed in the store opened up and welcomed Riley inside. She couldn't really describe it. Just like suddenly the light changed. Or the air seemed less oppressive. Or all the tables and piles of stuff no longer felt quite so overwhelmingly claustrophobic.

Something in the building decided she was allowed to be here now.

Which was an absurd thought. The *building* wouldn't care if she was here or not. The owners had decided to hire her. That was all. And she had decided to take the job. Nothing more.

She was feeling relief. Relief that she wouldn't end up homeless. Nothing else had changed.

She folded up her wool coat and tucked it under the counter where Doreen showed her an empty space. Then she rolled up the sleeves of her button-down and started to straighten tables and restack the stock that had scattered.

She didn't ask what had happened to the man who'd been there earlier. She didn't ask about the glowing eye in the center of the glass jar. She didn't ask about the way the storage room seemed to move and rearrange itself. She didn't ask anything at all.

Just cleaned up the floor alongside Doreen and Ian, and tried to ignore the feeling of being welcomed.

Mostly, because alongside the feeling of being welcomed, she also felt a vague sense of unease and foreboding. A sense that maybe this was a bad idea. Maybe this wasn't the…safest place to work.

The sense of being welcomed closed in around her, crowding out those worries. She was here now. This would be good. She'd work hard. Earn her pay. No problem at all.

This would be good.

She belonged here now.

ANGER MANAGEMENT

A DEMON HUNTER STORY

CHAPTER ONE

Quinn stalked into the pool hall, her attention focused on the meeting to come. She wasn't entirely pleased to be here.

The bar was dark, smokey. The sounds of pool balls bouncing off the felt lined table sides or cracking against each other echoed in the low-ceilinged room. The hum of men talking. The stench of too many sweaty bodies and stale alcohol ground into the ratty, rough wood floors over the years. Made her nose twitch. Not exactly a biker bar. Just a local pool hall. But dim and smokey enough to let the patrons feel a little dark and dangerous.

She kept her expression neutral but internally, she was rolling her eyes. So typical.

The only good thing about the place was the low rock and roll music paying in the background. At least it wasn't country music. She hated country music.

As she scanned the room, her gaze passed over the eight or so tables lit bright by hanging lamps and searched into the darker corners of the main floor. A man stepped into her path. She looked up at him.

A big man, though not particularly thick. Tallish, taller than her by a few inches, and wide enough in the shoulders. Brown hair a little long and slicked back. Clean shaven. Probably in his late thirties, early forties. Pale skin made whiter under the glare from the hanging light over the nearest pool table. He was dressed in slacks and a button-downed shirt with the sleeves rolled up. He smelled like beer and cigarettes.

She resisted wrinkling her nose, but barely.

He smiled. She stared. Waiting.

"Hey, beautiful," he said.

She continued to stare.

"Don't talk?"

"Do you have something to say to me?"

"You're real pretty."

She went back to staring.

He stepped closer. "Aren't you gonna say thank you?"

"For what?"

His sneering smile hardened. "I just gave you a compliment. You should be polite."

"You're an absolute stranger to me, and you think your assessment of my looks is worthy of my time, energy, or gratitude? Why?"

"Kind of a little bitch, aren't you?"

"Move," she said, bored with the exchange. She had a purpose here tonight, and this guy wasn't it.

"You should be nicer to me," he said, an edge in his tone now. "You don't know who I am."

"You don't know who I am either." She was already looking past him. Where the hell was—?

Quinn shifted her gaze back to the man when he crowded closer to her, getting into her space. She didn't move back, but she did have to tilt her head up to see into his eyes.

"You don't smile?" he said. "I'm just trying to be friendly here."

Another man at the table behind him chuckled.

"No," she said.

"No to the smile?"

"No to you being friendly."

"You should sm—"

She cut him off with a sharp hand gesture, pointing a finger at him like she might an ill-mannered dog. "If you tell me to smile, I will put my fist through your throat."

His lip lifted in a snarl, a sneer as he made a show of looking her up and down, taking in her height and size. "Smile," he finished. "You'd be prettier if you smiled."

She held his gaze for two beats. Then snapped out her hand, snatching him around the throat, squeezing hard. She lifted him, one-handed, up enough that his toes barely touched the floor. She continued to hold his gaze as he scrambled at her wrist, his fingers digging at hers. Her expression never changing.

"Because you're very young and stupid," she said quietly, her tone even, "I won't put my fist through your throat this time." She pulled him close, putting his face in hers. Even though that gave him better footing, her grip was hard enough he still couldn't breathe or stand steadily. "But you should be careful who you try to intimidate and threaten."

"Wasn't…threatening," he choked out.

"No. You aren't threatening to me. But you were attempting to be. You were trying to intimidate me and thought your size was enough. It was a bad idea."

She lowered her voice, her heartbeat steady and calm as she dragged him a little closer and tightened her grip on his throat. He choked and his face turned an ugly shade of red.

"Lucky for you," she said, "I'm older, and wiser. You'll

survive this encounter. Back in the day, you might not have. But never tell another human being again what they should do with their face. And don't assume you have the advantage because of that vulnerable dangly bit between your legs. You will be wrong more often than you think."

His fingers scratched harder at her hand. A pointless attempt to loosen her hold.

"If you do this again," she said, her voice even quieter, the tenor deepening with each word, "with anyone at all, I won't be as restrained. I will rip out your throat and calmly wipe my bloody hands off on your clothes as you die. Understand?"

His eyes started to roll back into his head but he managed a nod.

She tossed him aside. He crashed into the nearest pool table, then crumbled to the ground, gasping in air, his hand at his throat.

One of the other men came forward to tend to his friend as she turned her back on them both and moved toward the rear of the room, still hunting the shadows for the person she was supposed to be meeting here.

"How the fuck she gonna know?" the man who'd come to help her erstwhile intimidator murmured.

"I'll know," she said, her own voice carrying in the now quiet bar.

"She fucking heard that?" the second man hissed.

She allowed a very very slight smile before continuing her search of the faces scrambling away from her. She frowned at the deep shadows of what appeared to be an empty corner of the room.

She blinked and a woman stood there, leaning against the wall, her hands in the pockets of her jeans, her head tilted down just a little, though her gaze was focused on Quinn. And she was smiling.

Quinn shook her head as she approached. "I hate that invisible, suddenly appearing trick," she said.

"Interesting entrance." The woman nodded back toward the place where the man Quinn had nearly choked was now climbing, with a lot of help, to his feet. "Way to stay inconspicuous."

Quinn shrugged. "He was in my way."

"Noticed." Aidan pushed away from the wall, straightening to her full height.

She wasn't particularly tall. But not short either. She wasn't thin, or fat. She wasn't extremely pretty, but also not close to ugly. She was…ordinary. As ordinary as a human could get. Her plain brown hair was pulled back into a low bun. She wore jeans and a t-shirt that weren't particularly noteworthy. Her brown hiking boots were scuffed. Her pale skin without blemish or lines, but her age was vaguely… average. Not old. Not young. Somewhere in the middle but impossible to tell for sure.

And if you didn't look very closely, if you didn't know what you were seeing, you'd assume that flash of red in the depths of her very ordinary brown eyes was just a trick of the light.

"Why did you ask me here?" Quinn said.

"Need a favor. You were the closest."

"What the hell does a demon hunter need from me?"

The hunter smiled, and it was an ordinary smile, too. "I need you to bring me into the dungeon."

CHAPTER TWO

Quinn wasn't an actual vampire. Her mother had been turned—voluntarily—when she was pregnant and didn't know she was pregnant. Most pregnancies didn't survive the conversion. And once converted, vampires only reproduced by conversion, not by the human reproductive process of combining egg and sperm. Vampires no longer had viable egg and sperm for that type of reproduction. There was a modern idea that vampires with sperm could impregnate humans who had viable eggs, but if it had ever really happened in the history of vampires, no one had evidence or direct knowledge of it. Given how long vampires lived, if any of the old ones had witnessed such a thing, the rest of the community would know about it.

As far as most were concerned, a full vampire breeding with a full human and producing actual living offspring was a myth. A story told by humans, probably to explain pregnancies that were…unexpected.

Which was why only a very small number of dhampir, like Quinn, actually existed in the world.

They were almost always products of chance.

Conversions that happened while a future vampire was pregnant. Sometimes, on purpose. Mostly, not. And difficult to accomplish either way. Quinn supposed there were people doing research nowadays on the genetics of dhampir and how they managed to survive the conversion in utero. Some dhampir were probably curious enough to participate in the research. But she wasn't all that interested in the whys of it. She was what she was and that was all she needed to know.

What she was was as strong as a vampire and almost as fast, though her mesmerism skills were weaker, and she had no telekinetic abilities to speak of. But she could walk around during the day and maintain her superior strength. Vampires, in daylight, were more human in strength and speed. Their mesmerism still worked, if they were strong enough, but most of their primary abilities, most of the things that made them vampires, came out at night. So most vampires only came out at night.

Quinn didn't have that limit.

She also didn't need to drink blood very often. Maybe once every six months or so. And then she only needed a sip here and there. Even full vampires didn't need to kill to survive. They'd have wiped the human population out long ago if that were the case. Or been driven extinct by humans in a bid to survive their plague. But vampires required blood regularly and in higher quantities than Quinn needed.

And sometimes, they just liked to kill.

Quinn could kill. And had. More often when she was young, and brash, and angry. Actually, she was still angry most of the time. But she controlled that anger a *lot* better now. Which was why the irritating human man had ended up flat on his ass with his throat still intact.

She didn't hang out with vampires much either. She still had contact with her mother—a surprisingly good relationship considering—and had access to her mother's hive because the Master of that hive had been the one to convert her mother and had a soft spot for her, and by extension Quinn. But she didn't live in the hive, and she didn't spend a lot of time there.

The dungeon was not the hive. The hive was where the vampires lived and were safely hidden from homicidal human vampire killers who thought the idea of driving vampires extinct was noble. The hive remained safe so long as the Master vampire in charge kept their vampires controlled, not killing too much to draw attention, not converting too many vampires to be sustained by local human populations, that kind of thing.

The dungeon was a different place all together.

Not the kind of place she would have expected a demon hunter to want access to.

"Why the dungeon?" Quinn asked. "What don't I know?"

"One of the vampires has been making deals with a demon," Aidan said. "And he's about to lose control of that relationship."

That was…not normal. "Vampires don't make 'deals' with demons. Why would they?"

Sometimes vampires worked with demons. It was rare, but happened. They made alliances. Not bargains in the sense that Aidan was implying. Bargains were what humans did with demons to get something—usually power or health or wealth or some other such human concern—and the demon got whatever it asked for in return. And if the human didn't have the will to contain the demon they summoned, the human usually ended up dead and the demon set loose on the human realm.

That's where the demon hunters came in. They had the will to defeat a demon, send it back to its realm. No one could kill a demon. She wasn't even sure a demon could die, but if they could, they couldn't be killed by mere humans, even demon hunter humans. But a demon hunter could defeat them and force them out of this realm. If a hunter was lucky and very good, they caught the demon before it escaped, maybe even saved the human summoner from a horrible death. That was the aim anyway, according to Aidan.

Quinn had never really understood why they cared if the human survived or not.

But then she'd always had a low tolerance for most humans. To be fair, she had very little tolerance for vampires either. While she was welcome in the hive, because of her mother, she didn't like to hang out there. Vampire politics irritated the hell out of her and tempted her back to her more violent impulses just to get the dumb motherfuckers to stop all the infighting.

That thought struck her as interesting given what Aidan had just told her. "Do you know *why* a vampire is summoning a demon?"

It seemed an absurd thing for a vampire to do. They had their own strengths for infighting, their own weaknesses they wouldn't want exposed to a demon, and a distain for appearing weak in the face of other beings. But given the internal politics of the hive, it maybe wasn't as impossible as she might have thought. One of the weaker vampires might aspire to a greater, more powerful position through the help of a demon. Vampires had all been humans at one point. They still had all the foibles and failings of humans, just dialed up to eleven and with a great deal more power with which to exploit those failings.

Aidan shrugged. "Won't really know till I get there. Doesn't matter to my job, really. The whys. Just that the demons don't get loose. And there's a demon about to get loose. I need to get into the dungeon."

"You could have just gone in."

While Aidan might not be a vampire herself, she was a legendary demon hunter. And demon hunters didn't have the same…vulnerabilities to vampires as ordinary humans did. It was all about their will. A demon hunter had to have a will greater than a demon's. If they didn't, they died. So a living demon hunter was a hunter with a will to be reckoned with. Even by vampires.

"Faster this way. Don't have a lot of time to waste on…negotiation."

Quinn snorted. It was always ceremony and politics and machinations with vampires. Nothing straightforward and direct.

"Fair, that," she acknowledged. "They don't like me at the dungeon either, though."

"But you can get in, with fewer complications."

She wasn't asking a question so Quinn didn't bother to answer. "Let's go to the dungeon, then." She chuckled. "This should be fun."

CHAPTER THREE

Walking into the dungeon with a demon hunter was, as it happened, pretty fun. The noise, the chatter, the denials and anger. Quinn sort of liked watching them all panic. And the panic was exasperated by the hunter being accompanied by a dhampir.

The vampires were…uncomfortable around her. They had good reason. She remained strong and fast and deadly when they themselves were vulnerable. They couldn't kill her—oh, well, physically they might be able to. She, like a full vampire, wasn't absolutely immortal. She could die. She was just extremely hard to kill. As hard as a vampire, but with fewer periods of weakness to exploit.

And these vampires, the members of this hive, were forbidden from attempting to kill her by their Master. Because of the Master's fondness for her mother. That made them even more uncomfortable around her.

It was rather delicious.

The dungeon was, as one might expect, a dark place buried deep underground at the very edge of the city. Unlike the hive, which was set up for living and sleeping and all the politics of vampire life hidden away from the human world, the dungeon wasn't a place for resting. It was a place for play and excess. Full of indulgence and glut.

And a place they were allowed to bring humans.

Their food. Their play things. They were welcome into the dungeon and used here for all the things vampires liked to use humans for. Sex, blood, pets, entertainment. Whatever fit their fancy. The dungeon was where they could bring and use these human pets without risking the hive. And where the consensual-ish torture was allowed.

The only rule was that no one died. Dead humans drew attention. Vampires might be more powerful than humans, but there were a lot more humans in the world. And vampires were weak during the day. For everyone concerned, staying under human radar was better. And that was easier to do if the bodies weren't piling up.

The dungeon was arranged into several large rooms, built like concrete bunkers but decorated like a gaudy Goth French Versailles. The main room was swathed in black. Black silk embroidered material covered couches and chairs, thick black velvet curtains hung in front of pretend windows, black leather accented black lacquered tables, and the dark wood covering the floors was polished to near black. There were even a few black marble columns against the walls to really add to the opulence. The only colors in the room were spots of bright red—flowers, a lamp shade, a vase filled with red glass bobbles.

It was probably the most clichéd vampire place Quinn had ever been.

The other rooms were no better. Black leather and lace and silk decorated walls to hide the concrete, the furniture was all dark polished wood or lacquered in black. The spots of red vanished in some rooms, stood out in others. Even the torture room with all its toys carried the same motif, with cuffs and spikes and chains all painted a muted black. To be fair, that did hide the blood better.

Still, it was always a bit much for Quinn. The resistance to anything modern or anything with a color besides red in the dungeon struck her as too much playacting. Vampires were all about drama, all about the image, she supposed. And since humans were allowed here, they played into human myths as much as their own.

The scent of vampire permeated the place as well. A low level of musty dryness mixed with blood and the very faint hint of rot. As a dhampir, her sense of smell was almost as good as a vampire's, which meant the stench of so many vampires in one place was chokingly obvious to her. The humans sprawled around the main room, too nonsensical to notice Quinn and Aidan's entrance, didn't seem bothered, and probably didn't pick up the scent anyway.

Aidan stood in the middle of the main room, looking around at all the yellow-eyed vampires staring back at her. She didn't make eye contact with any of them, but Quinn knew, from firsthand experience, Aidan could meet a vampire's gaze and not get sucked in. She'd will herself to resist and so she would. A demon hunter's will was a pretty awesome thing to witness in action. Almost like magic. Except they didn't have magic. They just had a powerful enough will to make things happen that others couldn't do.

Like resist a vampire's mesmerism. Or slow their blood flow down and thicken it to the consistency of mud so a vampire couldn't drink. Things ordinary humans wouldn't survive.

She supposed if your life was fending off demons, vampires were just…another type of demon. But that got into territory Quinn chose not to entertain. Mostly because of her mother.

"Where to?" she asked Aidan as the faint whispers of unease and anger started to filter through the room. A hissing undercurrent. Words that either tried to seduce or drive away. None of it had any effect on Aidan at all.

The hunter paused for a long moment, her gaze unfocused, then, "This way."

She headed toward the back of the room, toward a door that led to what the vampires called the "breakroom." If memory served, it was just an open, empty storage room, but with hidden wall nooks so vampires could sleep if they were caught out in the dungeon when the sun rose. There wouldn't be anyone in there at this time of night. Normally.

They were halfway to the door when three vampires stepped into their path. Two men and a woman. One man dressed in a black leather suit, with even his tie made of thick leather, the other in a simple pair of black slacks and a black silk shirt with the sleeves rolled up over his forearms. The woman was wrapped in translucent black veils with strips of black silk that didn't hide the fact that she was naked beneath the dress. Two of the three where pale white, their skin practically see-through. They hadn't fed yet tonight. The third, the man with the casual slacks and button-down shirt, was of a darker skin tone, and his vampirically glossy black skin had enough life and silkiness to show he'd fed and fed well just recently.

He was also the one who spoke. "A hunter in the dungeon? Quinn, you brought us a treat."

Aidan smiled and met the man's gaze. Quinn kept her expression neutral. She didn't answer the vampire. Just stared at him, giving nothing away. For some reason, they expected her to be more reactive, more snarly. But her anger had always taken the form of a dead stare, right up until she ripped someone's throat out.

The man in the leather suit shifted from one foot to the other. A very subtle move that most wouldn't notice. Quinn did, without having to look directly at him. That one was nervous.

As well he should be.

The leader—a vampire named Perseus—let his dark-eyed gaze move between her and Aidan. No yellow glow in his eyes. He was in control and, for now at least, not attempting to threaten them. The two standing behind him, however, had let their eyes go yellow, the jaundiced glow a contrast to their pale pale skin.

Perseus smiled back at Aidan. "I'll ask your business once, hunter."

"I'll tell you once," Aidan said, sounding calm, though her gaze did dart to the breakroom door. "You're about to have a demon let loose on this party. And I'm going to stop that from happening."

"Vampires don't summon demons," Perseus said.

Aidan raised her brows. "What makes you think that?"

Quinn had had the same reaction. She could barely conceive of a reason a vampire might want to summon a demon. But Aidan's response made it sound like this wasn't a rare, first time thing. That vampires had summoned demons more than once in the history of vampires.

And that was an interesting fact.

She filed it away as she waited for Perseus to move.

He didn't. The two behind him glanced in the direction Aidan had looked. The door to the breakroom. The tension in the air went up, enough for Quinn to feel it on her skin.

She didn't change expressions, but she shifted her attention to the two lacky vampires. They weren't as controlled as Perseus. Younger, though not young, but nervous. She couldn't place their names. There were enough vampires in the hive, they'd blended together over the years. She really only cared about her mother and the Master, and only the Master because he determined her mother's fate. The others were…peripheral. She knew Perseus because he was old and strong, and the Master used him frequently to keep the others in line. She had probably seen the woman and other man before. She didn't sense them as newborns. But they were members of a background hum. Scenery. Extras on the set. No one she usually worried about.

Except that now, they were giving away hints in their subtle movements. Hints that things were not as they should be in the dungeon. And that was interesting, too.

She kept half her attention on them, the other half on the door to the breakroom. Mostly ignoring Perseus's continued interrogation of Aidan. Aidan didn't flinch or show much reverence to the vampire. She didn't show any fear either. She just stood there talking to him while most of her attention was on the breakroom door.

Her matter-of-fact tone must have bothered Perseus, though. Or maybe it was her disregard of his position. Because he took a threatening step toward her.

Quinn started to place herself in front of the vampires, to protect the hunter. She wasn't sure why she bothered. Aidan could handle a vampire—had handled vampires before. Still, watching Perseus come up against a hunter's will was almost as startling for Quinn as it was for Perseus.

Aidan turned the full force of her attention on him as he neared, met his gaze, and said, "No."

And Perseus just stopped in place like he'd hit a wall.

Like he'd come up against a shield. Except Aidan didn't have shields. That wasn't the sort of thing hunters did. Shields came with magic, with spells, with objects powered by magic. This wasn't that.

Perseus snarled, just a little, just enough to reveal the tips of his very white fangs. A slight hint of yellow flared into his dark eyes.

"I have a demon to stop," Aidan said, her voice quiet and calm. "We can continue this conversation later."

She moved around the three vampires as if they weren't a threat—which to her they weren't—and hurried to the breakroom. Quinn watched the two lacky vampires' gazes jump between Perseus and Aidan, and Quinn could smell their uncertainty. That was…not usual. They rarely revealed that much of themselves through smell. Weakness in a hive could get you killed. And other vampires would smell this uncertainty.

When Perseus looked directly at her again, she shrugged. "Demon hunter business," she said. "You'd rather the demon got loose in here?"

There were humans and vampires all over the place. A demon would make an absolute feast of all these beings. The vampires might think they were strong enough to overcome a demon.

Quinn knew differently.

Perseus snarled. "The Master will hear of this."

"Of course he will. He hears of everything." She tilted her head to study him. "He *does* hear of everything," she said more quietly. "Does he know that you know a demon is being summoned in his dungeon?" She couldn't imagine the Master would approve. It would constitute a threat to his power.

And maybe that was the point.

The two lacky vampires cast another nervous glance at

Perseus. Perseus snarled at her. A few yards away, Aidan shoved open the breakroom door.

The red glow inside was impossible to mistake if you'd seen it before.

A demon was here.

CHAPTER FOUR

Quinn walked away from the three vampires, giving them her back, as she went to help Aidan. Though, she was certain Aidan could control the demon—she'd seen her do some very impressive things in the past—there was at least one vampire in that room. One who'd summoned the demon. Quinn could at least keep that one away from the hunter while she worked.

Perseus grabbed at her arm as she passed, his grip strong enough to stop her.

She turned to face him. Met his gaze.

"You should never have brought a hunter here," he hissed. Now his eyes glowed full yellow, like the other two, and he brought his face very close to hers. His jaw had elongated, his fangs peaked out from between his lips. His fingers on her arm clenched hard enough to crush bone if she'd been human.

"Why?" she asked, her tone as neutral as her expression.

"This is none of her concern," Perseus said.

"You knew," Quinn guessed. "Your plan? Or someone else's?"

Perseus's grip tightened. "You are not part of the hive. This has nothing to do with you."

She took hold of his wrist, pressed her fingers in deep until she felt his fingers twitch, then twisted. His hand came away from her arm, despite his snarling resistance. She kept her fingers pressing into the nerves in his wrist and held him a moment, not flinching when he revealed his fangs fully. He thrust his head toward her, getting so close their noses practically touched. She didn't move, or loosen her hold on his wrist.

"You want your mother to survive this," Perseus said, "you'll stop the hunter."

"You touch my mother, I'll rip your throat out before the next sunrise."

Her mother was a strong vampire. An old one now. But Perseus was stronger. And older. And that could mean trouble for her mother. Because her mother was one of the Master's preferred, she was mostly protected from these political machinations. Perseus would only risk touching her, risk the Master's anger, if he thought the Master's anger was about to be made irrelevant.

"What did you offer the demon?" Quinn said, her voice quiet. "Who did you offer the demon?"

Perseus snarled again. The two vampires behind him closed in around her, circling her in a blink, moving at that speed that made vampires blur. She couldn't move quite that fast. Faster than a human, but not quite as fast as a vampire. And it was the middle of the night. They were at the height of their powers.

She kept her gaze on Perseus, but she was acutely aware of the other two, one just behind her, the other behind and to her right. Between her and the breakroom.

Where Aidan had just gone.

"You're in my way," Quinn said.

"Stay out of this," Perseus said. "If you won't stop the hunter, she'll die, and we'll finish this. But you will not interfere."

"I've promised the Master not to kill his vampires unless I have to. Are you going to make me have to?"

Perseus chuckled, but his cheek muscle ticked. A tell. He was old enough and strong enough to have more control over his expression than the ones behind her. She found his tell interesting.

She could hear the very slight shift of position by the vampires behind her. She didn't take her eyes off Perseus.

"You can't kill all of us." He gestured at the rest of the vampires. "Not in front of humans either." This he said in a very quiet voice.

"Is that why here? Humans to provide you some cover? Or because the Master never comes here, so he's not likely to realize what you're up to?"

Perseus's cheek muscle twitched again.

She didn't see his signal to the others. But she supposed they were going to attack even without a signal.

There was no getting around the fight with vampires sometimes.

Most vampires didn't bother learning how to fight properly. They used strength and speed and saw no need for anything beyond that. And most of the time, they were right. Strength and speed were enough.

But a dhampir in a vampire's hive needed some extra tricks up her sleeve.

So Quinn had trained to fight. Properly. And for years. The training had been good for her honing her anger, of course, controlling and properly channeling it. But all that practice also gave her an advantage with vampires in the dead of night when they were at their strongest.

Most of her mother's hive knew this about her. It was yet another reason she was mostly safe among these vampires.

But apparently, Perseus didn't understand what her training amounted to in a fight. Or he was just desperate to get rid of her and not thinking.

She only moved once they did, reacting to the swings, the grabs, the slashing teeth and nails. Waiting and watching as they threw themselves at her in an unorganized whoosh of violence. She could move almost as fast as they did, and her reaction time was better. The muscle memory there waiting for her, so she didn't have to waste time thinking.

A vampire threw itself at her. She blocked the teeth with a shove to the face. Another threw a punch. She caught his hand and squeezed enough to break bones before tossing him to the side. The woman came at her, trying to duck under a punch. Quinn stepped to the side and shoved again, sending the woman careening into a small lacquered table.

Noise from the breakroom shrieked through the main room, a piercing screech that wasn't a sound either humans or vampires normally made.

Quinn spun toward the door, took a punch to the side of her head that made her ears ring, and turned to face the vampire who'd just punched her.

She shook her head, then snapped her arm out and grabbed the vampire by the throat, picking him up and tossing him halfway across the main room. Aidan needed help. She didn't have time for these games anymore.

The humans around the main room started to stand and edge toward the elevator that led to the street level. The vampires either kept close to their food, or started toward Quinn.

She really didn't have time for this sort of fight. Too many vampires. And only one of her. Not odds she liked. Especially for a fight she needed to be done with quickly.

Instead of engaging, she made a sprint toward the breakroom. The move was sudden enough, and apparently unexpected enough, she made it to the door before Perseus caught her.

His hand on her arm squeezed so hard she was going to have bruises, and if she'd been human, he'd have snapped her bone.

"Do not interfere," he hissed. His eyes fully yellow, the irises elongating like a cat's eye. "This is not your concern."

"My friend is in there. I'm going to help her. And if you don't get your hand off me, I'm going to put my fist through your face." In truth, she'd been wanting to do just that to someone since earlier in the evening, and if Perseus wasn't careful, he'd be the unhappy recipient of her unleashed anger.

Slowly, deliberately, he released her arm. Then snapped a hand up, palm out toward the growing throng of vampires behind them, stopping them in their tracks.

"You want to…help?" He smiled, wide enough to show his fangs. "Be my guest."

She narrowed her eyes. He obviously thought she didn't know what she was running into.

Little did he know.

She pushed through the breakroom door, the red glow and heat from inside washing over her in a breath-stealing wave.

Gasps from behind her proved the vampires hadn't been expecting the heat either. And since vampires and fire didn't mix well, Quinn was sure more than a few of them had moved well away from the breakroom.

Nothing mixed well with fire—at least not anything that didn't want to die—so moving into a blaze always struck her as so counter to self-preservation instincts, no one in their right mind should do it. The fact that there was a whole field of humans who purposefully went into the blaze to save people and property always awed her—and very few things that humans did awed her.

The things Aidan did managed to, though.

It took long moments for her light sensitive eyes to adjust to the bright red and orange glow inside the room. When they did, she saw Aidan's silhouette against a huge shape that was made of the fire. The demon was a pretty classic example of the species. This one's body looked to be a moving human skeleton, the fire making up the "flesh." It's eyes glowed white hot inside those flames. There were horns sticking out from the skull, the only part of it not vaguely human-shaped. It's flame covered limbs were weirdly long in proportion to the rest of the body, giving it an almost gangly appearance, almost awkward.

Aidan was just standing there, staring up at the beast, and the beast stared down at Aidan, a staring contest Quinn knew was more than just a staring contest.

Demon hunter fights were strange things to witness. So much of them weren't visible. Not like a normal fight, with fists and weapons. Sometimes those things were involved. Aidan had a protégé who used a sword and used it well. But as often as not, the fights were silent tests of will, the battle taking place on a plane most observers wouldn't see. That left many to assume the demon hunter was losing, maybe captured by a demon spell.

They were always wrong.

CHAPTER FIVE

Quinn scanned the room for the vampire or vampires who'd summoned the demon. There was a chalk circle on the floor, and a pentagon inside with candles set at the points. The candles were black except for a red one at a point to the left of Aidan. Quinn followed a line from that candle to the wall and finally spotted…

Well, the blackened, steaming remains of someone. She'd have to ask later who that had been. But the vampire who'd done the summoning was dead. A husk of burnt flesh and charred bones now.

Quinn sighed. That was how demons escaped. That was why dealing with demons was stupid. They found the loopholes in their deals, killed the person who'd summoned them, and escaped to cause chaos. That was their entire purpose in their immortal lives. At least according to the demon hunters.

Quinn found it a bit limiting. To live that long and their only motive was chaos? Chaos was easy. Chaos was everywhere anyway, just needing a single flick to get started.

That wasn't impressive to her. Calming chaos? Forcing the world into something resembling order out of that chaos? That was impressive.

Which was probably why she'd answered Aidan's request to meet her at the bar. She admired the hunter and what the hunters did. Despite herself.

She inched over to the corpse. Killing a vampire was a lot harder than most thought, even by fire, and it was entirely possible this vampire wasn't dead. They deserved to be, summoning a demon like this, but if they weren't she should help. At least determine if they were truly dead or not.

There was noise from the doorway. She looked back in time to see Perseus slip into the room, his two lackeys standing just outside the door, blocking the escape. Those two stared up at the demon, seemingly frozen in place. Quinn didn't see vampires show their surprise often, so the looks of wide-eyed shock and fear on the two vampires were pretty funny.

Perseus barely looked at the demon. His focus was on the hunter.

Quinn snarled. He couldn't just stay the fuck out of this. She shook her head and raced into place between him and Aidan.

Aidan didn't react at all to either the new vampires or to Quinn. She continued to hold the demon's gaze. The demon seemed too focused on Aidan to notice the others in the room either.

One less thing, Quinn thought as she concentrated on Perseus.

"Out of the way," he hissed. "You have no idea what you're involved in."

"Stopping demon conjuring deals to overthrow the Master, I'd think."

He snarled. "You don't know anything."

"I know I'm not letting you stop the hunter from doing her job." She gestured at the probably-dead vampire against the wall. "The demon got one of your hive already. Are you really sacrificing so many, including humans, for a power play?"

"You don't know anything," he repeated, moving closer to her.

"You think I don't. That's why you sent me in here. You thought I'd step right into the way of the demon and get killed. My anger doesn't make me impulsively stupid." At least not anymore. There was a time in her youth… "It just makes me dangerous," she finished. "To the people who piss me off."

"Are you threatening me, Quinn?"

"Returning the favor?" she remarked, keeping her expression neutral and unaffected. An expression she was so used to after dealing with vampires and their manipulations her whole life, she wasn't even sure she knew how to express her feelings with her expression. At least not spontaneously.

"The demon needs sacrifice," Perseus said, his voice low. "We all knew that going in."

"All, huh?" She glanced at the charred remains against the wall. "Did they know? Or were they set up to be a sacrifice?" And did Perseus know that the summoner being killed released the demon without control into this realm? Or did he think he'd still control the demon somehow?

Perseus stepped closer and she snapped out a hand and picked him up off the ground by his throat. He wasn't expecting the move, the suddenness and her seeming inattention to what he was doing worked in her favor. Perseus wasn't weak or as bad a fighter as some of the others. But he was overconfident.

She used his momentary surprise and tossed him back toward the door. Then used the two seconds it would take before he returned to study the area around the demon. The chalked circle and interior pentagram didn't seem to have been disturbed. The demon was still *inside* the circle. The candles were still in place. And Aidan was firmly outside the circle as she silently fought the demon's will.

Still trapped, then. Quinn hoped. She didn't have will to fight a demon with. Only her anger. And frankly, she didn't think her anger was worth shit against a demon's fire. Not the flaming skeleton inside that circle anyway. Hard to beat up something physically when it could incinerate you the moment you tried to touch it.

Perseus returned within the predicted two seconds, his speed and recovery a lot more rapid than the other vampires. He wasn't a Master, she wasn't sure why he was trying to overthrow the current one—and the fact that he could only do so with a demon's help proved he wasn't strong enough to lead the hive anyway—but he was still strong and fast and smart enough to be the Master's right hand. Which meant she couldn't underestimate him or assume she could surprise him again.

The fact that he was still even trying to talk to her, to talk her out of interfering instead of just attacking her himself was…

Something she should consider more closely.

He put himself in her face in a blink. But he didn't attack her. Still. Just snarled and bared his teeth.

"Why?" she murmured.

"Why what? Why overthrow a Master who's grown weak and craven?"

"You're all weak and craven in your own ways," she said, still quietly. The sound of her voice faint under the roar of the demon's fire body. Still, with vampire hearing, Perseus wouldn't miss a word. "But you aren't strong enough to hold the hive alone. You wouldn't need a demon if you were. More than one of you is involved. Why?"

"You aren't part of the hive. You don't know what he's like," Perseus said. "If you'd just listen, you'd understand."

"You haven't tried to tell me anything yet," she pointed out. "Just repeatedly told me not to interfere. Threatened my mother's life. Sicced your people on me when I arrived to help stop a disaster. But not once have you tried to explain."

"There's no time, and it's none of your business."

"You said if I just listened I'd understand. Then tell me there's no time to explain. Except there is time. Aidan has the demon handled."

Perseus looked past her, frowning at the silent, unmoving "fight."

"He's caught her. She'll be dead in moments." He spoke firmly, but Quinn still heard the uncertainty.

"You really don't know what you're doing, do you?" She sighed. He was older than her by several centuries. Why was she the one who understood the world better than he did? "You've never seen a demon hunter fight? Never seen a real hunter at work?"

"You have?"

"She's my acquaintance for a reason."

"When? Why?"

"Long story. Not the point. Why have you summoned a demon into the hive that will kill everyone? You think that thing will be in your control if it overcomes Aidan? If its will is stronger than hers, you're fucked. All of you. Why would you do that? Why not just go to a different hive, a different Master?"

"No Masters," Perseus hissed. "No more. Don't you get it? The Masters are the problem."

"They're the way a hive works. The center that holds it all together."

Like a queen in a bee hive, they were the *reason* for vampires to exist. They moved around the Master like bees moved around a queen. And they did what they were told or else. Her mother had told her this repeatedly over the years, in explanation for why she didn't leave the hive so she and Quinn could live on their own. Vampires rarely lived outside a hive. There was safety in numbers, even with all the manipulation and machinations inherent in hive life, it was still safer. A secure location to sleep. People to keep you fed if something went wrong. A Master who ensured the human world didn't encroach. The monetary resources to live alongside a world that required them, even for vampires. According to her mother, the hive was the point for vampires, their family. Even the abusive ones were better than none.

So her mother said.

Quinn didn't believe that last part for a moment.

And apparently, she'd missed the signs of abuse if Perseus was willing to go this far.

"What has he done that you hate so much?" she asked. "Why all this to overthrow him?"

The demon's fire roared behind them, filling the silence that had settled over the room. The vampires hovering in the doorway didn't come into the room, just stood there as if to prevent those inside from leaving. Strange since no one who was in the room wanted out until the demon was vanquished —or in Perseus's case, until it was free.

But if it got free of Aidan while they were all standing around, they were all dead.

"How do you not understand that the demon will kill you and everyone else? That you'll have no control over it if it's free? Why on earth have you done this?"

She didn't understand any of it. And that lack of understanding, and his refusal to explain, were making her anger rise, pushing at her control.

Perseus stared at her for a long moment, his yellow eyes flickering with reflected fire light from the demon behind her. She felt the heat across her back, sweat trickled down her spine beneath her t-shirt and beaded at her hairline. Perseus showed no signs of sweat from the heat, his body didn't sweat—another difference between her and a vampire—but that flickering redness against his yellow eyes was eerie and full of heat all its own.

She blinked and Perseus attacked. No sign. No warning. Just launched at her throat, his long fingers tipped with sharp sharp nails going for her carotid arteries. His teeth bared.

She didn't have enough warning to avoid his attack all together. She was able to slip to one side, avoid his sharp nails, but his lunge still caught her across the side of her head and sent her flying hard into the ground.

He flew at her again even as she rolled away, and for several seconds, she barely stayed beyond his attack. Perseus wasn't one of his minions. He had some training. And now that he was using that against Quinn, she realized he'd hidden his skills all these centuries. Never shown her just what he could do.

Shit.

She dove away again, when he leapt into the air and dropped to the ground where she'd been, landing with a thud on the dark, almost black wooden floor. He hissed at her, showing his fangs, and scrambled across the floor to her before she could regain her balance and stand. He ended up on top of her, pinning her down.

She snarled. Punched him in the side of his face, which knocked his head back and lifted him enough, she got room to move her arms better. She grabbed his arms as he reached for her, shifted her position on the ground, and rolled, taking Perseus with her.

They rolled, scrambling at each other, an awkward and violent struggle to get purchase, to get the upper hand. His anger and violence nearly matched her own. But her confusion fed her anger and made it worse. She always got angrier when she didn't understand something. His attack, this demon issue, all of it just enraged her.

And she fought with more anger and less control than she had in years.

Perseus met her attack with his own violence unleashed. He didn't let up. Even when she punched him in the throat hard enough to break his windpipe. The injury slowed him down, but vampires didn't need to breathe like a human—or a dhampir. So a throat injury like she'd given him was less effective on vampires than it would have been on a human.

Something she knew. But she was fighting on instinct and anger, not logic and training now. Just so much anger she screamed with it, loosed it all on Perseus. He'd endangered all these people. All these humans. Her mother.

And he wouldn't tell her *why*.

She roared again, all rage and frustration as she threw punch after punch at his face, breaking his nose, cracking his jaw. He punched back and she took a shattered collarbone that also broke his hand.

Those injuries had them launching apart from each other, leaving several yards between them as their bodies rapidly healed from the breaks. She kept her injured side still while it healed so the break would knit back together cleanly and not leave her with residual issues.

Perseus stared hard at her, also holding still. He could have attacked again, even with a broken hand. He should have. Taken advantage of her injury and pushed his advantage.

When he didn't, she narrowed her eyes and again her frustration fed her rage. "Why are you doing this?" she snarled. "Why the demon? Why are you attacking me? Why are you courting a disaster like this? And why aren't you pushing your advantage?"

The frustration and confusion were a solid thing in her stomach, churning and harsh.

Perseus didn't snarl at her. He just stared.

"Tell me?" she yelled. "Why?"

"It's the only way," he finally said.

"Only way for what?"

He didn't answer. He just stared at her, his expression as dead as hers usually was, as emotionless. Telling her nothing. Just a blank stare and the flickering of red flames in his yellow eyes.

And then he attacked again.

Her healing bone made her movements slower. She turned away, prepared to take his punch on her uninjured side, but he didn't throw a punch or push her or even reach for her throat. He slammed into her hard with his whole body, pushing her across the floor.

She scrambled to push back, but he had the momentum. And with an extra punch of strength, he shoved her back so hard, she stumbled and flipped backward, throwing herself away from him and spinning around to land in a crouch, still facing him.

He stood at his full height and stared at her as she stared

back. She rose, slowly.

"I'm sorry," he said. "But it's the only way. Demons need sacrifice."

She blinked. Looked around.

Fuck. She was inside the containment circle.

And the demon had turned away from Aidan to face her.

CHAPTER SIX

Quinn, for all her dhampir speed and strength, for all the anger feeding that strength most of her life, was not in any way, shape, or form a demon hunter. Demon hunters required wills of steel. Wills that could overcome a demon's. Quinn was not that person.

Which meant her ability to fight a demon was sorely lacking.

No skill, no fighting technique, no speed or strength would save her from the fire if it touched her. She'd immolate as quickly as the vampire against the wall. And her chances of surviving that were worse than the vampire's. She could survive a lot. Complete immolation, not so much.

The demon rose up to its full height, its horns scraping the ceiling as the fire that danced around its skeletal body brushed the wood and whispered quietly in the silence. Silence that set Quinn's teeth on edge.

She'd been tossed into the containment circle. If she crossed back out, would it collapse and free the demon? Could she run back out? She was fast. Probably faster than a

"

demon. But if she left the circle, from this side, would that break it and free the beast?

"Aidan?" she asked into the quiet, her voice low and full of all the questions she wanted to ask but didn't have the focus to say aloud.

"Yup," Aidan said, as if answering all those questions.

Quinn didn't much like the sound of those answers, though. Sounded a lot like, "You're fucked."

"What now?" she asked Aidan.

"Now you die," the demon answered. "My sacrifice."

Quinn didn't respond to that. She was too busy controlling her anger at Perseus, so she could think. That rage she'd unleashed earlier wouldn't do her any good here.

The demon reached for her. And with no strategic thought whatsoever, she ran, circling around behind the beast at top speed.

It stumbled forward a step and spun back to face her.

She watched its white-hot eyes grow smaller as if it narrowed them, but the skull bones that made up its head couldn't do that so she wasn't sure how it accomplished the trick.

It reached for her again. And again, she ran. This time ducking beneath the sweep of fire as the beast's hand dove perilously close to her.

The sound of roaring fire filled the room. The stench of demon sulfur clogged her nose, making it impossible to smell the hunter or other vampires beyond the doorway. She wasn't a shifter, but her scene of smell was strong, and being without it was as disorienting as being without her speed would have been.

She risked a glance away from the demon for a split second, long enough to see Perseus confronting Aidan but no other vampires inside the breakroom.

She couldn't blame the other vampires. She didn't want to be in this room with the demon either. But more, she didn't want to be inside this containment circle. Especially knowing —or at least being pretty sure—that if she tried to leave and save herself, she'd free the beast.

Another sweeping grab by the demon focused her full attention on it. She couldn't help Aidan right now. Her only chance was to stay away from the demon long enough, survive long enough, for Aidan to do…whatever the hell it was she could do to stop the creature.

"You can run all you like, sacrifice," the demon said. "But I will not tire or wear out. I will eventually capture you. And eat you. Or you will try to save your own life by breaking the circle. Which will free me. And then I will eat all of you."

She wasn't squeamish about the word "eat" being thrown around in relation to her, or the other vampires for that matter. It was part of her world. Still, it sounded much more painful and infinitely worse when a demon talked about it.

Probably its point. Drive her crazy with fear so she ran.

She was pretty disappointed when she realized its ploy was working. The fear had her glancing repeatedly toward the door, toward the exit and safety. Escape.

She didn't run away much. Running went so against her instincts, her mother had had to teach her how to run away and retreat when it was necessary. Otherwise, she'd always been a stand-and-fight kind of person. Even as a child.

She very much wanted to run now.

Later, she'd wonder if that was a demon thing, a vampire thing, or a her thing. Right now, she had to focus on staying *inside* the circle with the demon so it didn't escape, while also not falling victim to the demon's touch.

Did demon fire burn like real flames? The ceiling wasn't catching fire, despite the demon's horns repeatedly brushing the plaster-covered concrete. The wood-covered floor wasn't catching fire either. If the demon's flames burned like regular ones, it should have already started a fire in the building.

Or maybe something about the containment circle prevented that?

A containment circle kept the demon in a hybrid state between its own realm and this one, but not *in* this realm. It was still, technically more inside its own than in hers while in the circle. Only breaking the circle allowed it fully into her realm.

So…did that mean she was in a demon realm while inside the circle or in her own?

Being sorely lacking in demon knowledge—because why the hell would she have needed a lot of it prior to this moment?—felt like a huge disadvantage. She wondered if Perseus had any of these answers, if he'd bothered to research before starting this… Whatever the hell it was supposed to accomplish.

She dove way from another swinging hand of flame, felt the heat roll over her head, heard the sounds of that roaring fire too close to her ears, echoing in her head.

The roll gave her a view of Aidan. She needed the hunter's help here. But just as she was about to call her name, Perseus attacked the hunter in a blur of motion…

And Aidan seemed to disappear.

Perseus stopped, coming to such an abrupt halt that if he'd have been a normal human that would have caused him a whiplash injury. He stood still and looked around, searching the shadows, his scowl fierce.

Quinn might have laughed if the demon hadn't swung at her again, drawing her complete focus—and fear.

Another swinging demon limb, another roll to the opposite side of the circle. Quinn had to scramble not to leave the circle this time. There wasn't actually a barrier to her moving in and out she realized suddenly as her hand landed directly on the chalk circle. A bare smudge at just the edge of the circle had her heart pounding.

Was that enough to weaken the circle? Enough to free the demon?

She'd expected, once inside, to be unable to leave the space easily. But it wasn't a barrier designed for her. It was only to contain the demon. Nothing to keep her from leaping out, even on accident.

The point. She knew. Her running away or dying. Either way, the demon and Perseus got what they wanted. Still, for some reason, the *ease* of being able to leave the circle startled her.

And made her slow.

The demon's hand swiped her, catching her off guard and sending her rolling to the other edge of the circle. Rolling too fast.

She stopped herself the way Perseus had stopped, with the sort of abrupt stillness that would have made a human hurt themselves. Actually, she wasn't sure a human could have stopped that suddenly. She had significantly more control of her body than a human did—except of course the hunters. But even with all that, she still stopped only a few inches from the edge of the circle.

So. That was the game?

She wasn't on fire. She wasn't burning from that swipe of demon flame. But the knock would have sent her out of the circle if she hadn't stopped herself. If the demon couldn't scare her into running away and breaking the barrier. It was going to just…knock her through the edge and break it open.

Not. Good.

She spotted Aidan again, this time in another part of the

room. Perseus saw her at the same moment and charged in a blur a human wouldn't have seen. Not even the blur of him. But before he reached Aidan, she had disappeared again.

The trick was wild and too much like magic. Quinn knew it wasn't magic. Just will. Willing those around her to no longer see her.

The things a demon hunter did with will…

Quinn didn't have time to see where Aidan appeared next or what Perseus did about the fact that she'd disappeared again. The demon charged, this time with its head down, like a bull, its horns directed at her. It had even dropped from standing on its back legs like a human to its hands and knees in a more bull-like posture. It's flame shroud bones seemed to have shifted as well, so it didn't look like a human on its hands and knees. It looked like a four-legged animal. Running head down.

Right at her.

She waited until the beast was within scorching distance, until she could feel its flames licking over her skin, before she pushed herself into a roll that took her under it. The flame's heat washed over her, choking her, stealing her breath, coating her throat in the sulfuric stench of demon.

But the move wasn't something the creature could counter quickly in its bull-shape. It couldn't just reach back with a convenient hand to grab her as she raced beneath it to the other side of the circle.

She rolled clear and rose to her feet to face it.

Knowing she couldn't do this all night.

She could go on for a while. She wasn't burdened with a human's lack of stamina. But she couldn't continue indefinitely. She needed Aidan's help—Aidan's knowledge! —and until Perseus left her alone, Aidan couldn't do anything for Quinn.

Which she supposed was the point.

So when Aidan suddenly appeared next to her at the edge of the circle, for the first time in Quinn's long life, she actually let out a sound like a startled squeak. It wasn't a noise she'd ever made before and later she was sure she'd be embarrassed.

In that moment, she was just relieved for the brief chance to ask questions. Or at least one question. The most important question.

"I know I'm fucked, but any advice on getting out of this without ending up dead?"

"Gotta deal with the vampire first," Aidan said. "He's persistent."

Quinn scowled.

"Keep ducking. I'll be back to help. Don't leave the circle."

Quinn opened her mouth to make a sarcastic comment on that last admonishment, but Aidan disappeared, and a second later Perseus was there. Quinn took a moment to snarl at him but didn't wait for him to speak.

Couldn't. Because the demon charged her like a bull again and she had to dive away.

She'd never done the bull fighting in Spain—she didn't like the way the bulls were treated, and while some humans might view that as a strange stance for a dhampir, she thought those humans who participated in the bull fights were barbaric—but she felt like she was in a bull fight now, and without the knowledge to get out of it.

She needed a…what were they called? She could only think of rodeo clown. But that term applied, too. She needed a rodeo clown to distract the demon bull so she could think long enough to escape.

It occurred to her after her next dive away from the bull

that *she* was the rodeo clown here. Distracting the demon while Aidan and Perseus worked out their differences.

She grunted as she rolled to her feet to face the demon's ass while it reoriented for another charge. Being the rodeo clown in this situation, when no one had prepared her for it, sucked big time.

Rather than charge again, the demon once again changed its shape, the skeleton inside the fire creaking, and sounds like breaking bone set Quinn's teeth on edge. When the transformation was complete—in mere moments—the demon was once again vaguely human-shaped, but its limbs were longer, its hands bigger.

And it now held a sword.

Because of course it did.

Quinn didn't have a weapon to match the demon's newly introduced sword made of flame-covered metal. Her weapon—the demon hunter—was occupied with an asshole vampire. Now what?

The crackling of demon flame inside the breakroom echoed so loudly she couldn't hear anything else anymore. Not the fight between Aidan and Perseus, not the vampires just outside the room blocking the door, not the vampires and humans—if there were any left—occupying the main room. Her whole world at that moment was the demon, its deadly flames, and figuring out how to remain inside the circle so she didn't accidentally loose the beast while not getting killed herself.

She supposed she could try to set a bargain with the demon, but that way lay all kinds of trouble. There were always loopholes in demon bargains and she was just as likely to get killed and release the bastard if she bargained as if she just continued trying to dodge it.

She slid under an arching swipe of the sword and straightened to her feet again behind the beast.

Bargaining also meant she had something she wanted from the demon, and at that moment, all she wanted from the demon was for it to stop trying to kill her and to go away.

Another dive to the left of the circle. Too close to the edge. Shit.

She wanted to save…well, not the hive necessarily. Having a Master vampire's protection had been useful all these years. Meant she didn't have to fight other hives constantly just to exist. But if Perseus hadn't been lying—and that wasn't a foregone conclusion—he'd implied an abusive dynamic in the hive. Which, to be fair, wasn't unusual either. The vampires usually sorted it out when a new Master killed the old one and took over. They didn't call in demons to help.

Leap over the sword as it swiped low over the ground. Too close to the fire that time. Jumping bonfires wasn't her thing.

She wanted her mother out of the situation, though. If it was a bad one. Even though the Master favored her mother. Had created her mother. That didn't mean he was good for her mother. And Quinn didn't want her mother to be destroyed in a fight other people had instigated.

Drop and roll suddenly. Sword inches from her head. Coming up too close to the edge of the circle again. A candle at one of the pentagram's points wobbled. She paused to stabilize it.

For a moment, her mind cleared just enough to wonder if her mother was involved in all this. Was on Perseus's side of this fight. If so, why not tell Quinn? Why keep her in the dark?

Sword thrust right at her chest. Last minute spin to one side. Away from the candle, which wobbled again but didn't fall.

Her mother might have thought she was protecting Quinn

by not telling her about the infighting and the coup attempt using a demon's aid. Something her mother would definitely do. Attempting to protect her while simultaneously, if accidentally, putting her in more danger.

Another thrust. Harder to dodge than the swings. Slip to one side. Another thrust. Slide to the other side.

Whether her mother was involved or not, though, bringing a demon into vampire politics seemed horribly short sighted for creatures that lived centuries. Without a Master to replace their current one, the hive would be vulnerable to other hives—with or without a demon. And if the demon was freed to kill their current Master, there was no reason for the demon not to decimate the entire hive. There just wasn't. Once free, the bargain it had set didn't bind it anymore, because it had found the loophole out of the bargain in order to escape.

Fast run behind the demon. Short breather before it turned and swung its sword at her again.

She just couldn't work out the end game here. The *reason* for all this. There were other ways. Better ways. Negotiate with another Master. Combine hives if necessary. Bring in a nomadic Master, or invite a Master from another hive that had more than one—the Master of that hive would likely jump at a chance to rid themselves of a competitor in their midst.

Dive and roll over the top of the sword. Cringe at the demon's ear-splitting roar.

The noise was loud enough everyone in the room stood still for a second. And though she was only peripherally aware of them, Quinn knew the vampires outside had still, too.

She hoped the humans had been allowed to flee by now. The fewer humans involved in the coming massacre, the less the human authorities would even notice it. The better for any surviving members of the hive.

Human attention on these things was *always* bad for everyone involved.

She had to dive away again as another swipe of the flaming sword barreled toward her. When she regained her footing, Aidan was at the side of the circle waiting for her.

"This particular vampire is determined to keep me distracted," the hunter said.

"This is his plan. I'm not sure what the end result was supposed to be."

"Doesn't matter. I need to focus on the demon."

"Would help."

As they watched the demon raised its sword overhead. Quinn prepared to dodge again, but instead of bringing the sword down toward her, it sheathed the sword in an invisible scabbard on its back.

Hmm. That probably wasn't good.

"It's changing again," she murmured to Aidan.

"Yup. And that's gonna be bad."

"Not exactly happy-fun times up to now."

"If I toss the vampire in there with you, you can handle him?" Aidan hadn't taken her gaze off the demon.

"He'll just run out of the circle and break it to release the demon."

"Be your job to prevent that."

"While avoiding the demon?"

"Yup."

"That sounds…" She shrugged. Being able to beat on Perseus to release some of this fear while Aidan took care of the demon that Quinn couldn't beat on to release her fear sounded… "Fun."

Aidan snorted. "The vampire is determined."

"I'm pretty fucking irritated now. I'll be fine."

"Irritated." Aidan nodded, her gaze never leaving the demon as its bones began to rearrange themselves again. "Give me a minute."

"Not sure we have a full minute," Quinn said, but too late. Aidan was gone.

She knew Aidan didn't move at speeds equivalent to a vampire or a shifter. She couldn't just *be* somewhere else without having to physically move there at human speeds. But her will could ensure those around her *perceived* her change of position as happening faster than it did.

Demon hunter wills—well, Aidan's will at least—was a terrifying thing.

Quinn wasn't sure what she'd have done with a will like that. Mixed with all that inner anger she kept perpetually contained? Probably not a good mix. She might have brought down the world a long time ago.

The demon reached its new form.

This one definitely was…not good. Wings like a bat's only with flame instead of flesh covering the bones stretched the full length of the circle. It still had arms, though they were smaller in reach now. Its legs were short, bat-like limbs ending in clawed talon bones rather than human-like feet bones. And the center of its body had shrunk and thickened.

The resemblance to a bat, inside a vampire space, felt… deliberate. Maybe a little mocking. Quinn might have laughed and enjoyed the joke if she wasn't the one stuck inside the circle with the flaming bat.

The wings were so large, though, she wasn't sure what use they'd be inside the containment area. Then the demon moved the wings, creating a roaring hot burst of wind that very nearly pushed her past the circle's chalk line at her feet.

Ah. Yeah.

That wasn't good.

The heat and sulfur stench of the wind made her wince. She leaned in, putting herself closer to the demon's flaming body as it pumped its wings again and another burst of scorching wind blasted over her, scouring her exposed skin.

Her feet slid backward, despite her best efforts. She glanced down. Her heal was *on* the chalk.

She scrambled forward the instant she could, but that thick wind pummeled her again and she dropped to her hands and knees in an attempt to keep from being blasted right out of the circle.

Quinn had learned to do a lot of things with her strength over the years. But one thing she'd done since she was a kid, something she *hadn't* had to do much since she was a kid, was heavy her weight into the ground so she couldn't be moved. Making herself immovable had been interesting against vampires—especially ones like her mother who didn't want to hurt her, even when she was being a stubborn pain in the ass—and there'd been a few times she'd done the trick just to irritate a bully.

Push me, she'd dare them while defiantly staring at them in the eyes. They couldn't mesmerize her to get her to move. So they'd try to pick her up. And picking her up against her will was a lot harder to do than it should have been.

She might not have the will of a demon hunter. But she was stubborn beyond all measure. And if she refused to be moved, she wouldn't be.

So long as staying still didn't also get her caught on fire, she could hold her ground.

The wind blasted her and she heavied herself into the hardwood floor. It had been polished and smooth at one stage, but thanks to either the effects of being inside a containment circle or to the demon itself, the floor was now scuffed and rough under her palms. Which actually made the job of stubbornly *not* getting blown out of the circle easier. Being lower to the ground helped too.

The problem would come when the demon shifted from wind to attack. She waited for that switch, knowing in her gut it was coming, watching the beast's feet even as she refused to budge from her position, leaning into the wind as another blast of it washed over her.

Demons were fast, like snakes and gators, sudden and more agile than you might assume by their bulk. But they weren't vampire fast.

When the beast moved, so did Quinn, throwing herself under its now shorter, stubbier legs and to the opposite side of the circle. Fire singed her hair and right arm. She didn't think about that too close. Wounds healed. Anything short of full immolation and she'd survive, recover even. But thinking about going up in flames would slow her down. So she didn't.

The demon had to fold its wings against its body to turn, giving her precious time to reorient and face its next wing beat, the blast of furnace-hot wind scorching her, sandblasting her raw with its sulfur stench.

The beast screeched out a sound this time that was several octaves and a few decibels higher than its last roar. A disabling sound that forced her lower to the ground, hands over ears. That was the kind of noise that would pierce a vampire's skull. Hers wasn't faring much better.

The onslaught stopped so abruptly, Quinn practically rocked backward as the silence washed in.

She looked up, to see if she needed to move again or muscle down against another blast of wind.

And saw Perseus standing in the middle of the containment circle.

Under the demon's white-hot gaze.

CHAPTER EIGHT

ime was a funny thing for vampires and dhampirs alike—well, at least for her. She didn't know any other dhampirs. With centuries stretching out before you, moments fell away so quickly, even years sometimes, that she had to pause and really consider the time that had passed. The fact that this thing had happened a year ago, not last week. That this other thing had only happened three days ago, not deeper into the past. Time bent and twisted and filled in all the movements through her long life and quite often she didn't even notice it passing until she made an effort to look around and do some calculating.

Those frozen moments—after Perseus stood inside the circle, while the demon looked down at him, while Quinn crouched half the circle away—felt like the world had stopped spinning. She was used to the relentless march of time, the flow of it ever going. A moment when everything seemed to slow, come to a stop, pause as the true horror of the situation sank in... That was a new sensation.

She wasn't sure she liked it.

The demon reached for Perseus with its flame

enshrouded, taloned hand. Its wings spread as if it would sweep them forward, hitting the vampire with a blast of furnace-hot wind. Perseus narrowed his glowing yellow eyes up at the beast. The beast's white sun eyes in the middle of its skull flickered just slightly.

She had no idea what Perseus would attempt—did he think he had the will to stand against the demon?—but she couldn't wait to find out. If the demon tossed him outside the containment circle, the circle broke. If the demon killed him, the sacrifice was made and whatever bargain had been set was completed. If the demon was slow and Perseus ran out of the circle, the circle broke and released the demon.

All these options filtered through her mind in that brief, weirdly slow moment in time.

None of the possibilities were acceptable.

She raced toward Perseus, wrapping around him and spinning him to the ground just as the demon beat its wings and a blast of air so scorching she felt like her skin was flayed rushed across her back. She had a moment to breathe and wince and groan, and then Perseus rolled beneath her and grabbed at her, his teeth out.

Not even grateful for her help.

The anger at not understanding all this, at having to both defend this asshole so the demon didn't kill him and also keep him inside the circle so the demon didn't escape, all while he worked against her…

Her irritation morphed into a full-on rage. For a long time now, she'd reined in her rage and kept it under tight control. It wasn't something pretty she could turn loose in a controlled manner if she didn't hold tight to those reins. But this particular situation pushed her dangerously close to the edge of her control. She'd been slipping, letting her anger tease out, losing control by inches. Which only angered her more.

So she took her rage out on Perseus.

She didn't even wait for him to attack. He reached, his fingers curved into claws, his teeth lengthened in his mouth. But that was as close as he got to an attack. She roared, a sound to rival the demons, and punched Perseus in the face.

Ah! The crack of knuckles against bone and flesh. The satisfaction!

She let all the repressed anger surface, and she punched him again. And again. Face. Stomach. Anywhere she could reach while straddling him. He fought back, of course. But his prone position and their equally matched strength did him no favors. He might be willful and determined, and he might be full of his own anger…

But that was nothing to her inner rage.

All that rage spilled into her, out of her, as she beat on Perseus. He'd started this. He'd gotten another vampire killed. He'd been willing to sacrifice innocent humans. He let vampire politics and machinations get in the way of sense.

He'd tried to loose a demon on the world.

She punched and snarled and punched some more. He'd fed that night so her fist found blood. Blood that sprayed across her face when she connected just right with his nose. She felt the thick slide of it over her cheeks but ignored the sensation. She didn't need blood right now. She'd drank weeks ago but recently enough to be satisfied. She didn't feel the call of hunger.

No. Only the rage.

Perseus wasn't weak. He was a fighter, too. But her banked rage, let loose, overcame even his determination. He got in a few good hits. She'd have noticed the split lip, the broken ribs, the crack in her cheekbone in a normal fight. Now, all she felt was a vicious pleasure in finally being able to let loose all that anger on a worthy victim.

When Perseus stopped fighting back, when he lay under her half-conscious, she paused long enough to take a breath. A deep one. One that took the anger with it.

As fast as it had risen, the anger drained away. Her muscles were pleasantly tired. Her body felt sated. She'd need a nap soon. A nap sounded nice. She closed her eyes briefly and dropped her head back.

Remembered abruptly she was still inside a containment circle with a demon.

She launched off Perseus and landed in a crouch a few feet away, facing the heat, knowing the heat was the demon. She couldn't believe she'd closed her eyes! Forgotten what was happening around her. Where she was!

This was why she kept the anger banked. This was why she never let it fully out. It took over. It became her. And she stopped paying attention to the things that mattered. Like a still-very-dangerous demon only a few feet away.

Later, she told herself. She'd berate herself later.

To her relief, the demon wasn't paying any attention to her or Perseus, though. Its full attention was now on the hunter standing just outside the circle. Another silent battle. Or so Quinn assumed at first. Then she heard Aidan chanting.

The words were Latin, which struck Quinn as predictable, but there were words in there she hadn't heard in several centuries. Vampire words that weren't spoken aloud among outsiders. And hadn't been used in her hive in so long, she wasn't sure any of the young vampires knew the language. The vampire language had been used, once upon a time, as a necessary way to remain secret. When vampires had refused to adapt to the human world in order to hide in it.

Now, they hid better. Sometimes in plain sight. And the language had fallen away, only taught to new turns out of tradition—a tradition that had also been dropped in some hives. Like hers.

Yet Aidan stood at the edge of a demon containment circle and mixed that vampire language with Latin—an incongruously weird sounding mix since the vampire language contained sounds a human wouldn't be able to hear.

The demon reacted to the chant. It snarled and hissed. It had changed shapes again. Gone were the deadly fire wings and bat's body. Now it stood as the vaguely human-shaped skeleton she'd first seen when coming into the room. And it kept trying to reach through the circle to grab Aidan.

Aidan stared up at it without moving, repeating another refrain in the weird mix of vampire and Latin. The demon screeched, throwing its head back and covering the sides of its skull head where ears would be.

The gesture struck Quinn as strangely ordinary, even as she had to cover her own ears, hoping to keep the demon's scream from making her bleed.

The screech went on. Aidan didn't stop her chanting. She added in some hand gestures. And the way she moved her hands looked…wrong for a human. There was a sensuousness to it that seemed very vampiric. A slithering, undulating grace. Nothing in the hand movements made sense to Quinn. But they made even less sense coming from a human.

"She has to stop!" Perseus roared.

Quinn startled, realizing he'd not only recovered from his beating but was on his feet again.

She snarled and tackled him to the ground as he made a move toward Aidan. At vampire speed he'd reach the hunter in a blink, leaving the circle to do it. She couldn't let him get out. But she'd drained her rage on him already. She didn't have any left to turn loose. Not yet. Not now. Now all she had was determination.

Which she used to hold a struggling vampire on the ground. He was as strong as her physically. He fought off her hold. She fought back, ignoring the new scratches, the reopening of her split lip.

The demon's scream went up another octave and Quinn saw spots. The beast thrashed its head from side to side. Its skeletal shape shrank and expanded, like it was breathing with its whole body and the fire around it.

Outside the circle, Aidan raised her hands. She held a knife in one. Quinn only caught a brief glimpse of it before she had to focus on containing Perseus again. Where the hell had the knife come from?

Perseus grabbed her around the throat in her distraction, his sharp nails biting into her flesh. She tucked her chin to make choking her more difficult, and rather than scramble at his fingers, she slammed the sides of her hands against the inside of his extended elbows.

Between humans, the move would have made his elbows buckle, loosening his grip on her neck so she could break his hold. With her dhampir's strength behind the action, she broke Perseus's elbows. His roar matched the demons, in volume if not precisely pitch.

"They'll heal," she spat. "Stop fighting me. The demon has to go."

"You have no idea what you're doing," Perseus snarled.

His bones healed quickly. As she watched the odd angle of his forearms rearranged themselves to something more normal.

"You keep telling me that," she said. "You haven't told me why." Though she'd drained most of her inner rage, the lack of information did drive her frustration and anger back up again. Not like the earlier rage, but enough she felt that heat swirling in her chest again. "Why not just overthrow the Master like any other hive? Why call a fucking demon?"

"Because of you," Perseus shouted.

She leaned back. "What the hell do I have to do with all this?"

The demon roared again and this time Quinn thought her sensitive ears really would bleed. Blood dripped from Perseus's nose, whether from her having hit him earlier or from the demon scream, she wasn't sure.

As the demon's screech tipped up another head-splitting level, Aidan's voice somehow managed to carry over all the noise. That shouldn't have been possible, but still Quinn could hear the hunter chanting over the demon's scream. Strong. Sure. Full of her powerful will.

Quinn could actually feel her will at work. Maybe it was being inside the containment circle with the demon, this space meant to link it to its own realm and not allow it into theirs. Or maybe it was just that Aidan was that strong. Quinn didn't know—and was sure the hunter would never tell her— but she could *feel* the power of Aidan's compulsion... No. Her *command* that the demon return to its realm. That the demon remain there. That it not come back. Not tomorrow night. Not to the vampires. Ever again.

"Stop her!" Perseus shouted at Quinn, bunking under her in an attempt to dislodge her. "She has to stop. We need it! Do you know how long this took. What we had to do?"

"No," Quinn shouted back, settling her weight more solidly on his abdomen, keeping him pinned to the ground. "No, I'm not stopping her. No, I don't know what you did. Or why. What the hell does this have to do with me?"

"He will kill us all before allowing you to be in danger," Perseus snarled. "He chooses you over the safety of the hive.

He's made…arrangements with other hives, other Masters, so that no one will remove him from power. Deals…for you."

She didn't believe that. Not for a moment. The Master was…tolerant of her. But never showed her anything but tolerance. Her mother was a favorite. That much she knew. But Masters had favorites. Some favorites lasted many centuries before the Master got bored with that particular love and moved on to another.

But *she* was not one of the favorites. She just happened to be the offspring of one. And *she* did not belong in a vampire hive. She was the ultimate threat to one. Something the Master had told her.

Repeatedly.

She frowned down at Perseus. The Master had told her many times over the years, as she'd grown and strengthened, that she was dangerous to vampires. Their ultimate fear— someone with their strength and none of their weaknesses. This wasn't entirely true. And she'd had to discover that part on her own. But she was considered a threat to vampires in much of the dhampir lore.

"He's been using me as a threat to control you?" she asked. "He's been threatening you with me?"

"He does when it suits him. But that's not the main issue. He endangers us *all* by keeping you with us. He's used you to manipulate and intimidate other Masters. To make deals they can't refuse—or he'll send his dhampir in to destroy their hives."

She blinked. She wouldn't… Just for the hell of it. Just because the Master told her to.

For all her rage, and her violence in her youth…her ability and leanings toward violence now… She wasn't a cold-blooded murderer. And she wasn't the Master's executioner either. Not once, in all these years, had she killed for him. Ever.

Why the hell would they all think she *would*?

"The other hives we might turn to for help refuse," Perseus said. "They fear you. He uses that. To protect you. So he can keep threatening others *with* you."

"I've never killed for him," she murmured, knowing Perseus would hear her even over the demon's continued racket. Somehow, the demon, and Aidan's banishment of it, seemed less immediate.

"You don't have to for us to know you can."

"He can kill you as easily as me." Easier, really. He was their Master. He…controlled them. That was the exchange made for the safety of living in a hive. The Master was in charge and held life-or-death control of every part of a vampire's life. The Master didn't need her as a threat. Not against his own hive.

Against the other hives… Against another Master looking to overthrow him… That was different. She could see him using her as a threat against other Masters, other hives, even if she wasn't one—or at least not at the Master's pleasure. She hadn't known he was doing it. But she could believe that he did.

But against his own hive… Unnecessary.

"He keeps you all safe by ensuring no other Masters invade," she said.

"He keeps us prisoners. No options or ways out."

"You can leave the hive." That was always an option. Hives were safer. Vampires rarely left once settled with one. Finding one to commit to could take time. But once settled, they usually stayed. They *could* leave, though. Live alone. Move to another hive if the Master would take them. It happened.

Often enough in other hives, Quinn should have seen it happen in her mother's. At least once or twice. Probably more over the centuries.

She'd never known a vampire to leave this hive.

In hindsight, that seemed…unlikely.

"He uses me," she said, aloud.

But her voice got lost in the noise of the demon, a wail unlike anything previous.

She realized she'd stopped hearing its screech in the moments before the wail. Realized her ears had stopped hurting in those precious seconds. She'd been so deep in thought she'd have forgotten the noise anyway. But as this new, piercing sound ripped through her mind, the previous moments of silence sank in.

She faced the wailing beast, its flame body flailing from side to side. She ducked as its wild movements swung its arms over her. The circle suddenly felt even smaller, as if the beast swelled in its desperation to deny Aidan.

Quinn cursed. Fucking thing *was* growing. She pulled Perseus, without any help from him, closer to the edge of the circle, away from the demon's fire. But she kept between the chalked edge and Perseus so he couldn't cut the circle and free the demon. The position meant she had to keep one eye on the vampire even as she tried to watch the demon, and that split attention didn't leave her much room to think about what she'd just learned.

Perseus did lunge toward the circle's edge. She caught him around the neck and held him in a choke hold as she watched the end of the demon fight, shaking her head at him when he made a feeble attempt to dislodge her arm. He wasn't trying much anymore. She could feel the resignation in his body. It was night. He'd fed earlier. He was at full strength. But it seemed he'd drained what will he had to release the demon when he'd told her *why* they'd summoned the beast.

She still wasn't sure what they thought a freed demon would do for them. It might kill the Master. But it would kill the entire hive as well.

Perhaps that was the plan. Maybe they—or at least Perseus and a few of the vampires here—hadn't seen any other way out?

There were easier ways to die, though. Even for a vampire.

Aidan was no longer chanting. Quinn saw the knife clearly in her hands now. She'd cut her forearm at some point, and blood dripped from the wound onto the ground. More blood was on her finger tips and she drew a symbol in the air in front of the thrashing demon. The beast's skeletal shape had changed from vaguely human to something… something unlike a creature of this realm. Not one Quinn had ever seen before.

There were limbs, but more than four, and a tail with a spike, but it was short and didn't look good for much. The head was elongated, the horns still small and poking out of the top. There was the suggestion of a snout in the shape of the fire around its face, but also the suggestion of a wide mouth disproportionately sized compared to the skull. Claw-tipped appendages on the multiple limbs, some that looked like fingers, others like toes, others like talons. A set of wing bones had sprung from its hunched back, the flames giving a suggestion of bat wings again rather than feathered bird wings. But they were small and stubby compared to the body, almost like vestigial limbs.

It flailed as Aidan drew another symbol in front of it. And then her voice, deep and calm and steady beneath the roar of beast and fire, filled the breakroom, filling in all the spaces even though she wasn't shouting.

"You will return to your realm and not return here. There is no place for you here. Begone. Begone."

The demon lunged toward Aidan, a snake tongue made of fire emerged from its mouth, stabbing in her direction. The hunter didn't move. She repeated the "begone" and made one last hand gesture with her blood-covered finger tips.

The demon spun into a tight, whirling ball of fire and bone. The whistling sound of its movement hit octaves that reached even beyond Quinn's dhampiric hearing, but still managed to reach into her skull so she felt like she was the one spinning into oblivion.

And then the fire ball demon exploded, washing heat and flame through the circle.

CHAPTER NINE

Quinn ducked and rolled herself over the top of Perseus as the fire washed over their heads.

The heat was so intense that for a split second she thought they were both dead. The fire had finally caught them. Their bones were melting, their lungs roasting, their skin blackening and peeling away.

But in the next moment, cool air blew across her skin, taking the heat and sense of being cooked alive with it.

She blinked. She could see, though everything around her was darker than it had been.

Perseus moved beneath her, though barely, but enough she knew he was still there. Vampires didn't move much at the best of times unless there was a purpose to it. So she supposed his purpose was either to let her know he still existed and wasn't permanently dead, or he was about to attack.

Either way, she didn't feel like fighting much anymore, so she leapt away from him, landing at a part of the circle closer to Aidan.

Only to realize the circle was no longer chalked into the

wooden floor. No more circle or pentagram. Not even whisps of chalk to indicate where the lines had been. The only evidence anything had even been on the floor were the five grease stains that had once been candles.

"What's happened?" she asked Aidan quietly.

"Demon's gone," Aidan said with a shrug.

She looked so unbothered by the fight, Quinn shook her head. And here she thought *she'd* perfected the expressionless look. Well, it wasn't that Aidan looked expressionless. She had a sort of content, laid back, neutral expression that wasn't precisely pleased, but definitely not blank or emotionless either. Not relieved. Not horrified. Not really even phased.

It was a very confident and effective expression, whatever the hell it was and however the hell she managed it.

"Your vampire acquaintance okay?" Aidan asked, nodding to Perseus.

He was propped up on his elbow, staring blankly at a grease spot where a candle had been, his expression unreadable and truly expressionless. His eyes were still yellow in the darkness. But Quinn got nothing from the hard lines of his face. There was still blood from his smashed nose drying against his dark cheek, but he ignored it.

A reminder, though, that every injury she'd given him had healed now.

All the injuries he'd given her had healed as well.

"There's a problem in the hive," Quinn said quietly to Aidan.

"Got that impression. No real reason to summon a demon otherwise."

"Yeah, but it's not what I would have…expected."

"You gonna leave?"

The fact that Aidan asked that question meant she'd heard more, or just knew more, than Quinn had prior to this fight.

"I don't like being used as a threat to keep anyone where they don't want to be. The Master isn't mine."

"He's your mother's."

"Something I'll discuss with her. If she wants to stay, she's free to do so. But I don't have to." She wasn't really part of the hive. She'd only remained near it all these years because of her mother. She'd moved when the hive had moved to stay close to her mother. But for everyone's sake, it might be better if she went…elsewhere.

"Where?" Aidan asked.

"Not sure." She shrugged. Lot of places in the world. Plenty she hadn't seen yet, despite all these centuries on the planet. "I'll have to…negotiate my way around the other hives." There were places she wouldn't be welcomed. But she liked a good fight, so that didn't sound like a problem.

"He might kill your mother in revenge," Aidan pointed out quietly.

Perseus looked up at that, facing them for the first time.

Quinn didn't have to ask Aidan which "he" she meant. "My mother isn't a weak vampire. In body or mind. If she chooses to stay in this hive, she chooses so knowing the risk."

"He'll be overthrown if you leave," Perseus said. He didn't stand, or move other than that he was now looking at her and Aidan. "He won't last long without you."

"That's between him, his hive, and the other Masters. It should never have had anything to do with me."

Perseus didn't nod or acknowledge her comment with a gesture. But the…tension in the room lowered just enough she knew he wasn't going to charge her and try to kill her for ruining his demon plan.

"This'll work better," she said to him, loud enough to be clear to the other vampires still hovering just outside the breakroom door.

No one came inside. No one was close enough to the black hole of the door that she could see their yellow eyes anymore. It was pitch black beyond the door now, no longer any lights for humans to see by. The blackness didn't matter to vampires. Didn't matter to Quinn either. She wondered if Aidan had trouble seeing in this level of darkness, but if the hunter did, she didn't show any signs of discomfort with it.

"No freed demon rampaging through killing everyone," Aidan said with a pragmatic nod. "Typically, better for all involved."

Perseus's lip lifted. It was a sort of snarl. Maybe an attempt at a smile? It was hard to tell because nothing in his facial expression changed otherwise. The lip lift was almost like a tic that lasted longer than a moment before subsiding.

"You could have talked to me," Quinn said, her voice much lower now. "You could have…told me."

"Why?"

"I might have left sooner."

"You also might have told the Master and gotten me killed."

She sighed. Of course that's what he'd assume. Vampire politics and machinations were deadly. And a pain in her ass. She'd always preferred staying out of that mess.

She'd never have guessed she was at the center of the hive's disfunction all this time, without even knowing it.

"The sun will be up soon," Quinn said to Perseus. "I'll talk to my mother today. Leave before nightfall. The rest… That's between you all and the Master. Though, I might… discuss options with another Master before making a move."

That was the closest she was going to get to giving them advice. She was done with this hive. What happened next was up to them.

She did hope her mother was smart enough to survive it

all. She wasn't sure she'd call what was between her and her mother love. But not exactly *not* love either. Complicated. But not bad. And she'd prefer to have her mother still in the world rather than not.

"I'll keep her safe if I can," Perseus said, so quietly Quinn wasn't sure Aidan heard the comment at all. "If she allows."

Quinn nodded. Best she could hope for. Perseus wasn't a Master. He couldn't hold the hive together on his own. But he was strong, and old, and cagey. Clever enough to have kept this demon summoning business a secret from the Master. If any of the vampires in the hive could help her mother, it would be Perseus.

If her mother wanted the help.

"Things are going to get messy after you leave," Aidan said, her voice quiet, too. "You sure about this?"

"So long as they don't call any more demons, I'm good."

"Fair enough. And if they do summon any more demons, I'll know where to find them."

Quinn spared a glance toward the remains of the vampire near the wall. That one was definitely gone. An existence wasted, as far as Quinn could see.

She chose not to dwell on the thought. You had to make your choices and live with the results. Or die with them. Her mother had made a choice to turn vampire, and that choice had resulted in the unlikely existence of a dhampir daughter. She'd have never guessed the consequences of that choice would extend to all this. But here they were.

"Walk you out?" she said to Aidan.

Aidan shrug. "Sure." She glanced around. "I'm done here."

"It's not coming back?"

"Nope. Not that one anyway."

THEY MADE THEIR WAY BACK INTO THE EERILY SILENT MAIN room of the dungeon. No hissing. No obstacles in their path to the exit. The vampires melted away from them, blending into the shadows at the corners of the room, only their yellow eyes flickering like candlelight to indicate they were even there.

"Did you know?" Quinn asked quietly as they stepped into the lift that brought them up to street level. "When you contacted me, did you know?"

"Might have had a suspicion," Aidan said.

"How?"

"Instincts. Hard to explain. Comes with the job."

Quinn snorted. "Did you know how this would end?"

"Never know for sure."

"But you had a suspicion?"

Before the lift door closed, Quinn looked back over the main room. Perseus stood in the doorway of the breakroom, watching her leave. He didn't do anything human like wave goodbye, or even nod. She didn't wave or nod either.

Outside, in the fresh night air, Quinn pulled in a deep breath, letting the warm breeze clear away the stench of vampires and demons from her nose. "Where will you go now?" she asked Aidan.

Aidan contemplated the street, empty but for a few cars rolling past between red lights. The industrial area where the dungeon was located didn't have much night life or traffic. The building itself, from the outside, just looked like one of a dozen warehouses scattered throughout this section of town. Boring. Unoccupied. Definitely not the sort of place to house a den of vampires.

"Off to the next fight," Aidan said, her hushed voice

matching the quiet street. "Got a few days till it happens, though. You?"

"Not sure. Guess I'll decide after I talk to my mother."

"You did good in there," Aidan said. "Against a demon. Ever want to take up demon hunting let me know."

"No," Quinn said, very firmly. Aidan had made that suggestion before. Her answer was always the same. "Besides, demon fights are weird." And, at least in this case, had some very unintended results.

"Can be," Aidan said as she headed down the street, waving over her shoulder as she left. "Can be."

BURNING INSIDE A STONE CIRCLE

CHAPTER ONE

The heaters jittered and hissed in the background as Riana stared out the window at the falling snow, her stomach muscles tight, restlessly tugging on the edge of her sweater. White covered the open space in front of the cabin, painted the pine trees beyond, dusted the front porch. She smiled. Snow felt perfectly appropriate for today.

She pressed a hand to her stomach, trying to calm her nerves, and faced the small cabin.

The two-drawer wooden cabinet she used as an altar was set up near the unlit fireplace. She still needed to lay out the candles in their proper order, but the smooth stones in the wooden bowl and the small cut-crystal glass of water were ready and waiting for the ceremony to start. A fire in the fireplace might add ambiance. She was all about the ambiance today. Hell, even nature decided to add Her own decorative touch with the snowfall.

All the details in place and just right. Perfect for a transition day.

The mantel clock over the fireplace dinged once, it's gears moving visibly though its glass and wood case. Only two thirty. She had time. Her stomach growled, surprising her, and she chuckled.

"No food yet," she told it. "After the ceremony. Once the transition is over, we'll celebrate with the feast. But not yet."

Better to do the magic work she had ahead of her on an empty stomach. She hadn't always done that. In her Maiden days, she could eat without thought and often did, even before a magic working. The Mother days had changed a lot of that. Changed everything, really. Which was the point of the transitions.

The ceremony ahead, though, entailed a lot more… history. A lot of things she had to face, to accept. Things she wasn't sure she wanted to look at again. A lifetime of choices made, consequences lived… History. The previous two transitions hadn't had the weight of all those choices on them. The years as Mother had been complicated. Difficult. Challenging. Wonderful. She wouldn't have traded them. But they hadn't been easy.

Yet, here she was.

With Ann, her youngest, graduating from college finally, she felt… She wasn't sure. Accomplished was the wrong word. Satisfied? No, that was wrong, too. Proud? Of her children, absolutely. Not always of herself, though. Content? Maybe. Content was the closest emotion. Like she'd made it through a very tough few years to the other side, and the other side wasn't horrible. In fact, she rather liked this side of those years.

Thank the Goddess for that. There had been times in there when she couldn't see to this transition. When she'd worried she'd never make this particular place in life without burning the whole thing down. There was still a lot about those years she didn't want to revisit. Things that haunted her, but that she had to confront. Suppressing the memories would leave her heart less achy, but also leave her stuck in this place, unable to move on.

And it was time to move on.

For everyone's safety, including her own, she had to face this transition.

With a half hour until the ceremony, and too restless to just sit and wait, she pulled her puffer snow coat off the coat tree by the door, stepped into her calf-high snow boots, and headed outside. Seemed a shame to miss out on the glorious snowfall. If Nature wanted to celebrate this holiday with her, who was she to refuse?

The wraparound wooden porch had collected a light dusting of snow, though the overhang protected most of it, and the wood pile stacked up close to the door was covered in a waterproof tarp, so a fire in the fireplace was still an option. She pulled a wooly cap out of her coat pocket and dragged it down over her hair, hair gone silver over the last two years. The gesture reminded her strongly of her Maiden days, though. When she'd been young and full of defiance and fire. So full of fire she'd have melted the snow stepping out into it. But she'd had to go through the motions then. Had to hide some of herself, protect some of herself, to survive in the world.

She was really looking forward to not doing that. Ever again.

Stepping off the porch, the snow crunched under her boots, such a satisfying sound she took a few deliberately hard steps just to savor it. That reminded her of her kids, when they were young, playing in the snow over the winter holidays they'd spent up here. Rare and precious family time when the rest of the world wasn't demanding their attention. When she didn't have to argue with school authorities to ensure her oldest got the services she needed. When she didn't have to push and nag at her youngest just to get her to focus on something other than car racing and Lego sets. When her husband wasn't drained and grumpy from his job.

When they could be together without having to pretend to be other than they were.

Her favorite part, that. All of them being unabashedly themselves. No masking, no hiding, no pretending. Just… completely themselves. Glorious.

Dale in particular had needed that time away from the world and its expectations.

Riana had worked so hard not to impose societal expectations on her oldest child, but still Dale had developed masking skills to cope with school and being out in public, learning to curb her stemming behaviors, and keeping a lot of her rolling stream of talk about her favorite subjects to herself until she was home and could spill all that pent up information to her mother.

During those years, Riana had learned to listen in a way she'd never thought possible. And she was so grateful to Dale for that. Taught her a lot, her daughters. Both of them. Some of those lessons hard to learn. And oh so many mistakes she'd made. But all of it was important. Experiences she needed now.

Especially with this next, last transition upon her.

A milestone she was also so grateful to have reached.

She let the joy of the moment fill her, from her booted feet, through her gut and up into her chest, into her heart. Letting the sense of it spill over. She caught the faint glow of her aura brightening from the corner of her eyes, but that was fine. Up here, with no one else around, in the middle of the bright snow, she could glow without worry.

Speaking of masking skills.

She spun in a slow circle, arms wide, face turned toward

the gray sky as the snow drifted across her cheeks, melting against her eyelashes. She grinned, even opened her mouth to let some of the flakes fall onto her tongue. The sharp cold, the melting taste of fresh water, better than wine.

Though she had some good wine set aside for the feast that she was really looking forward to.

Cold air kissed her cheeks, gently nipped at the tip of her nose like a kiss. And that… That reminded her of the man still waiting for her at home. Someone she hadn't expected to find. Another part of the transition from Maiden to Mother that hadn't gone precisely as she'd planned. Yet, there was nothing about her life she'd change, and nothing about her time with Jacob she would want to have missed. Not even the fights. Not the close calls. Not the occasional loneliness. Not the mistakes. All of it had made a beautiful tapestry and removing one thread would destroy the entire thing.

No, with him, she'd accepted the tough stuff, because it had highlighted how very good the good moments were. One less thing to confront later. She hoped.

She glanced at the nearest pine tree, and because the thought amused her, she wrapped her arms around the thick trunk and gave the tree a hug. Hugging a tree. Her grandmother's irony meter would explode.

The rough bark scrapped against her cheek, the scent pine needle strong, and she felt the slowing flow of sap through the trunk, the quieting for winter, the settling into this next phase of life, the sleep before bursting forth in the spring to start all over again.

Cycles of life.

She headed back into the cabin, stomping her boots off on the rough doormat outside the door.

No more stalling. No more waiting. It was time to start.

CHAPTER TWO

nce Riana had shed her coat and boots, she took her place at her altar, sitting on the floor in front of the small cabinet. In her youth, she'd been able to do this sitting on the bare wood floor. But with age came both wisdom and more achy joints, so she used a small mediation pillow now.

The two drawers of her cabinet altar held most of her necessary paraphernalia, everything she required for any sort of witchy work she wanted to do. The cabinet was small enough to be portable and easy for her to move to different locations as well. The drawers were painted a dark blue and decorated in various star and moon symbols because those spoke to her. The back was painted green, with an elaborate tree carved into the paint.

For this ceremony, for the formal transition, the smoothly warn wooden top of the altar was spare. On purpose.

She said a small prayer to the Goddess and set a protective circle that enclosed her, the altar, and a clean and empty section of wood floor all around her. When she felt the circle close, saw the flare of blue light in her inner eye, she let out a slow breath, let the nerves that had followed her up the mountain and danced in her stomach all morning settle.

Her heartbeat steadied as her body relaxed into the magical space. Tingling energy moved over her skin. No going back now. Not that she would, even if she could.

She smiled.

Then she began.

She carefully placed the stones in a circle around their wood bowl, setting the crystal cup of water into the wooden bowl, arranging the candles at the four cardinal points around the square top of the altar. She faced the West, the direction of sunset, and had used a green candle in that directional position because it felt right. Most of her work, she did by feel and instinct. Some of the things passed down from her elders she used. But her grandmother ensured from the start that Riana understood her practice had to be personal or it wouldn't do her any good. The fire would consume her if she tried to adopt other people's processes.

This had to be hers and hers alone, or the transitions would fail.

Thus the smooth stones she'd collected over a lifetime because they were pretty or odd or interesting. And the cut-crystal glass because she'd bought it on her honeymoon in Ireland. And the wooden bowl passed down to her from her great-grandmother on her mother's side, the smooth oak dark from years of use.

Even the cabinet that served as her altar had been picked up at a yard sale and she'd refinished and painted it to suit herself.

She closed her eyes and allowed the inner fire to rise, the heat crawling over her skin, through her blood. In her inner eye, she saw it, a heat once so white it was almost blinding, now a beautiful red and orange glow. Still full of strength and passion, but *almost* fully in her control now. This next step would solidify that, giving her that final level of control she'd need to ensure she didn't accidentally set the world on fire.

Which was such a relief she was almost giddy.

But first she had to complete the transition. And face some of the things she didn't want to face.

Now came the delicate part, the potentially disastrous part. This was why the transition had to be made alone.

Well, physically alone anyway.

She murmured the spells, those ancient and passed down through her family for generations. Her husband's family wasn't a witchy clan, but her husband's grandmother had… dabbled, and never hesitated to participate in the important holidays and ceremonies because she was all about the family. The spells came from Riana's side, though. Some of the few things she brought into her practice that hadn't been changed or adjusted to suit her personal process. No, these she did precisely as originally written.

As she whispered the words, quiet even though she was the only person in the cabin, she let her mind go where it wanted to, where it needed to. Her memory brought her back to the time she'd gotten into a fight with a bully in middle school, the way she'd had to clench her fists to keep from unleashing her inner fire. A pile of dried leaves at the far end of the playground had started to smoke. The ensuing chaos of teachers stamping out the fire and getting the kids safely away had broken up the fight. Her bully left her alone after. But Riana had been shaken.

Her mother yelling at her for breaking a favorite coffee mug, because she was messing around with it. The way the shame had let the fire rise and she'd nearly set a curtain alight. Her mother's apology for yelling and the soothing moments Riana hadn't quite believed because if she hadn't accidentally lost control, her mother would have still been mad.

Her college years. The tears, from her and her mother, when her parents drove away, leaving her on her new campus. The first class, the humiliation by a teacher when Riana didn't know the answer to something she hadn't studied yet. The clenching fist and the tremor of fire under her skin. Maintained. No accidents. But close.

The abortion that left her relieved and grateful after a condom failed and panic had nearly stolen her burgeoning control. The few dates and short term relationships with people who weren't Jacob. Meeting Jacob. Falling in love.

The first transition.

Riana let out a breath slowly, letting that first period of time settle again, a part of her now. History she wouldn't change that led her forward. A first transition successfully made.

Then she began to speak the next part of the spell.

Again, the images rose without guidance.

Dale's birth, the pain in the moment nothing to the exhaustion and fear that followed. How could they let her leave the hospital with such a tiny, delicate being in her care? Didn't they know she had no idea what she was doing? Dale a fussy baby that didn't sleep well, and Riana a new mom whose inadequacies choked her. The candles she lit without touching them so she could control her fire without accidentally harming her beloved but difficult baby.

That moment, that one moment when she felt the control slipping, just a little. A moment she could barely face, even now, even with Dale grown and happy and successful.

The day she discovered she was pregnant with Ann, thrilled with the news. Overjoyed, but cautious, after the previous miscarriages. This one stuck though. This pregnancy brought her her stubborn, smart, beautiful youngest child. And still the fear on that day of discovery, the worry that this one wouldn't take. Again. The way she'd quietly lit a pile of papers on fire and tossed them into the fireplace so she could control her fear.

One of the hardest days. The hardest months. The day, when Dale was three, they'd been told she was autistic, and that all those dreams and hopes they'd had for her would have to be changed. The end of that month, after blaming herself, wondering what she'd done wrong despite *knowing* she'd done nothing and this was just who Dale was, realizing she was letting other people tell her how she was supposed to feel about her baby and her baby's future. Getting angry that other people were trying to force her into seeing her baby differently. Dale hadn't changed. Dale was who she was and had always been who she was. And Riana refused to let the outside world tell her otherwise. Her baby was brilliant and beautiful and would grow up to be a whole, wonderful person if Riana had any say in the matter. That moment, though, had left her so angry, she'd had to take a cold shower in the middle of the night to quench the flames.

The closest she'd come to losing control in years. Another moment she'd never forget.

More images, more moments from a long life, more moments when she might have let her anger out. The fight with Jacob where she'd actually burned the counter in the kitchen and had to lie to her daughters to explain it. The shame of the lies she told until they were old enough to understand. The fights with Dale during homework that led to meltdowns, moments that could still bring tears to Riana's eyes. Her failure to be as patient and accepting as her daughter needed her to be.

She felt those tears rolling down her cheeks as she moved to the next part of the spell.

The control held when she faced off against a school faculty who didn't want to provide Dale with her necessary accommodations. Control held when she got the job she wanted and the joy of it burst through her in light and heat, but no fire escaped. Control held when she and Jacob traveled together and bickered over the details even as they built joyful memories. Control held during the birthday party where he'd surprised her with a beloved puppy even though he was nervous around dogs, and her happiness nearly exploded from her.

More tears ran down Riana's cheeks. Her voice deepened. More words. A chant now. Tumbling out faster and faster.

Watching Ann leave for her first school dance, her beautiful daughter's glowing face as a very nervous boy walked her out to his mother's car. The heart-swelling pleasure of seeing Dale graduate high school and then college. Holding Jacob's hand tightly as they dropped Ann off at college. The relief and excitement when Ann moved to her new apartment and got out of a bad dorm situation.

New voices joined hers. Quiet at first. But Riana heard the echoes as the new voices layered into her own chant. Like a song. A choir.

And now started the hardest part. She stopped her own chant. The spells had been issued. The choir in the background would continue that part. Now was her time to face what she'd sent out into the world as Mother. Now all that came back three-fold, and she couldn't change those consequences.

But she let her heart focus on the good, as much as she could, on the joyous moments, not the anger, not the sadness. Not the regrets.

They came back anyway. The first punch of sadness hitting her like a train, taking her breath. The angry moments, the regret next, hard pummeling hits, almost physical they connected so hard. Each gut punch slamming against her, filling her chest with all the years, all the emotions. She forced her mind to the joys, to contented feelings, as they crashed into her as well. Three-fold. Intense and overwhelming. Tears leaked faster down her cheeks. She closed her eyes, absorbing it all. All of that part of her life, returning in wave after wave, building the intensity as it roared into her. Until her body felt tight, overfull, her skin about to split open from holding too much emotion.

The tingling of her inner fire covered her skin, hurt, like a sleeping limb waking. She tried to breathe through it all, tried to take it all in without losing control. The fire burned under her skin, in her bones, and she let that be, too. All of it was her. All of it was what she'd sent into the world. It was her responsibility to take it back in.

And then the guilt. So much guilt over those years. Not enough of her given. Too much. Too many angry moments. Too much distraction. Those moments when she should have been paying closer attention, should have *seen* them. All of them.

More tears. Sobs now too. Pain so deep she could no longer breathe around it.

The chanting in her head got louder, cooling the pain, the guilt. Enough that she could breathe again. She let the emotions run through her, opening to give them all the space they needed. And more of the pain eased. Breathing got that little bit easier.

Finally, the last emotion, the very last thing she had to face.

The last time, this one had almost cost her the transition.

The last emotion then had been her anger, her bone deep anger, the rage that fed her fire when she wasn't careful. She had so so much of it, for the injustices in the world, for the hateful, for the mean.

But as she waited for the three-fold backlash of her own anger, she realized she'd…felt that already. That had come earlier. So…

What was left?

The love washed in, then. Love for her husband and kids, yes. But also for her mother. Her sister, her grandmothers. Love for her neighbor who irritated the hell out of her even as he fixed random things in their garden without asking. Love for the teachers who'd helped Dale and Ann. Love for her dog and two cats. Love for her best friends.

The love rolled over her in such a fierce wave, she lost her breath again.

There were the friends she'd have never made it this far without. Her mentors, who kept her sane. Her colleagues, who had her back.

So much of the love she hadn't even realize she'd sent out, now all coming back to her.

Even with her eyes closed, she saw the glow that encompassed her, the bright white light that radiated from her skin. She felt the red-orange fire in her gut flickering and sparking, and it warmed her. Didn't burn. Didn't hurt. Didn't rage out of control. Like a campfire, the heat felt delicious and soothing. And she basked in all that warmth.

All the love.

The chanting choir in her mind quieted slowly.

Finally falling silent.

CHAPTER THREE

When Riana opened her eyes, their shadows were with her. She smiled.

Her maternal grandmother, Grandma Baker, stood to the left, her hands clasped in front of her. She was small and straight and softly rounded, her eyes glowed in the translucence of her shadow. Next to her, her daughter, Riana's mother, smiling. She was taller than her own mother, but as rounded and soft, a contented grandmother in her own right now.

On the right, her paternal grandmother, Gran Owen, joined in shadow, taller and thinner but more hunched at the shoulders. Her smile was bright, though, as she accepted a place in a celebration she hadn't grown up with, a holiday she'd embraced when her son married Riana's mother. Next to her, Riana's sister. Lisa was still in the height of her Mother period, had taken on found family and a collection of orphaned animals to care for and fiercely protect—the Mother didn't have to birth or raise children to be Mother. Lisa was years away from this transition, still, but Riana looked forward to that celebration when the time finally rolled around. She gave her sister's shadow a little finger wave before focusing on the two waiting just before her.

Her daughters.

Dale, tall and contained, narrowly built but full of accepting energy. She smiled, her eyes crinkling at the corners. Ann even taller than her older sister but less willowy, sturdy and solid—more so now that she'd gotten through her more difficult teenage years and those early twenties. Their shadows filled her with another wave of love, and she thought, *yes*. A good way to start this phase.

"Thanks for joining me," she said to the shadows of her loved ones.

"Wouldn't miss this celebration for anything," her mother said. "How do you feel?"

"Exhausted," she said, with feeling. That earned her a few chuckles and a snort of amusement from her Grandma Baker. "But good. Content."

"The fire?" Grandma asked.

"Warmly crackling over the wood as it burns safely inside a stone circle." That was the image of her fire in her heart and inner eye now. No bonfires. No raging sunbursts. Just a lovely, dancing campfire that kept her face and hands warmed.

Grandma sighed, her smile relieved.

Riana's mother patted Grandma Baker's shoulder, the movements familiar even in their shadow forms. "I almost couldn't make this transition," her mother said. "It was a close thing for me. I'm glad yours went so well."

Riana snorted. "Oh, it was hard. But…worth it, I think."

"A life fully lived, even with the ups and downs," Gran Owen said. "Always worth it."

Riana smiled, the contentment and exhaustion settling over her. "Thank you again for joining me."

"We'll be there in person in a few hours," her mother said. "Rest. Eat."

"Don't drink all the wine until we get there, though," her sister said.

Their shadows faded slowly, her daughter's shadows holding on a few moments longer.

"Dad's already waiting in the car," Ann said. "We'll be there in about an hour."

"Drive carefully," Riana said. "It's snowing."

Ann snorted and rolled her eyes. Riana gave her an unrepentant shrug. The transition didn't negate the other periods. She was still Maiden. And most definitely still Mother.

"Love you, mom," Dale said in her quiet voice.

"We love you," Ann said. "See you soon."

"See you soon. I love you."

She waited until all of the shadows had vanished. Then she went through the final part of the ceremony. She thanked all those who'd aided her working, the Goddess for attending her transition, the elements who'd joined her to see her through. One by one, she put out the candles, ending with the candle in the West. She replaced the rocks into their wooden bowl, the cut crystal glass of water next to the rocks once more.

She'd leave the altar this way for the rest of the day, during the feast, while she still glowed with the effects of the transition. A physical reminder she'd succeeded, she'd moved into this last phase, made this last transition.

And now, with a great deal of excitement, and even more acceptance of all that had come before, both good and bad, she finally got to be…

Crone.

THE MUSEUM OF SMALL ART'S EVERYMAN

CHAPTER ONE

he Museum of Small Art, located off the beaten track in SoHo, on a side road between clothing boutiques and hip restaurants, wasn't the usual place to host this kind of exhibit. Usually, the museum hosted exhibits of miniature paintings, small portraits, silhouettes, lockets, snuff boxes…anything and everything in miniature.

A touring exhibit of "the grotesque and cursed" would typically find its home in different types of museums. Places more gothic or Avant Garde. The Museum of Small Art was the kind of place school groups visited during holidays, and tourists sought out to say they'd been there. Not really the haunt of those seeking strange and creepy pieces.

But somehow this particular exhibition had found its way into the Museum of Small Art, for a limited time, and brought with it some truly grotesque paintings and sculptures.

None of which Anne Reynolds would have seen if not for the body in the middle of the main gallery.

She could have done without seeing either the exhibit or the body.

The bright, cheery outside of the museum, with its giant

purple banner announcing the name of the touring exhibition didn't quite jibe with the dark interior and the strangely uplit exhibits. Pools of light rose from the wooden floor to cast eerily moving shadows on white marble statues of demons, satyrs, and twisted monsters. That same light rose to illuminate paintings of torture, demon dances, and monsters munching on the helpless. There were depictions of Hell, vampire feasts, demon orgies, and a witch burning that gave Anne the shivers.

She definitely didn't need reminders that her kind had been burned at the stake not too long ago, historically speaking. And yes, "centuries" was still not that long ago for that kind of trauma.

To avoid thinking about the witch burnings, she focused on the body. The reason Detective Suarez had requested her presence.

The woman was young, maybe mid-twenties, white, slim build, with long dark brown hair, currently splayed across the polished wooden floor like wings. Anne chose not to look into her wide open eyes just yet, so she didn't know the color. Her arm was thrown out at a strange angle to her body, one leg bent under her, the other stretched wide. Like she'd been shoved backward. Or pulled from behind. She was dressed in jeans and a t-shirt with a unicorn on it, which was a stark contrast to the twisted look of horror on her face and the blood pooling under her body.

Somewhat to Anne's relief, outside of the sharply metallic scent of blood, the area mainly smelled like lemon cleaning polish and a strange undertone of some sort of flowery incense Anne couldn't put her finger on. She mostly worked with the police on fraud and forgery cases. She had a particular talent for uncovering forgeries—not least because she'd had some experience creating them—but also, it was how her psychic skills worked. The smell of paint thinner and canvas was a much more likely scent for her to encounter than bodily fluids. This was only her second murder scene. The first hadn't involved blood, though.

There was a lot of blood at this scene.

According to the museum director, Melissa James was one of the artists who regularly visited the museum to practice her skills by drawing the various paintings and some of the sculptures from the permanent exhibits. She was here most Saturdays, and had talked with some of the staff about her excitement for the touring exhibition as she'd heard about a particular painting she wanted to try recreating.

"Dr. Gilbert said she doesn't know where the victim worked or lived," Detective Suarez said, reading from a small notebook—which Anne knew was unnecessary. Suarez had an excellent memory for details.

"When was she found?"

"Ten a.m. when the director showed up to open the museum."

"Any idea how she was in here after hours?"

"If any of the staff allowed her to stay, no one is talking yet."

Anne nodded.

Not far from the body a three-legged plastic stool had been upended, and a large sketchbook flung opened, some of its pages folded, the top one ripped in half. Charcoal pencils scattered in a wide arc opposite to the body. There was a large canvas courier bag open near the sketch pad, which the police had already searched. The whole scene, body and scattered art supplies, were in front of a painting hung on a brick wall at the back of the gallery.

The painting was the sort of thing you had to look at a few times, and look at closely, to really see the strangeness of it. At a glance, it just looked like an ordinary portrait of a human man. The man was in profile so the viewer wasn't looking at him straight on. He wore a suit and bowler hat. The artist who'd painted him had given his skin a sort of pale gray cast, but that could also be the lighting. The background looked like a melting landscape of trees and a pond.

If you didn't stop to look closely at the painting, that was all you'd see. A relatively ordinary portrait with a vaguely rendered background.

But look closer…

Anne stepped carefully around the body. She wore a full body jumpsuit over her jeans and t-shirt, and her tennis shoes were covered in little blue booties so she didn't trample evidence on accident or muddy the crime scene in any way. Though she suspected most everything that needed to be collected had been collected. She was only called in after the forensic people had been through a scene. In this case, Detective Suarez had brought her in before the body was covered or removed. She was sure he had his reasons. She was sure he wanted her to do her thing with the body.

Most of her attention, however, was on the portrait.

Inside the ordinary image, there were…details. She stepped as close as she dared, careful of the body and the scattered pencils. Leaned close to the painting. But not too close. Because what was inside the picture…

The man's face was made up of tiny pale gray-skinned demons, dancing and cavorting, forked tongues, long claws, spiked tails, wings, tentacles for some limbs. There were so many of them, they jumbled on top of each other. Red and peach colors served to outline individuals and shade others, creating the depths of the face when standing back from the portrait. If she looked closely enough at all those little bodies, they seemed to actually move.

She blinked and turned her attention to the hat. Also demons, though these all blackish purple—skin and feathers and scales. The details of each illuminated by subtle red details and lines, a color that, at a distance, blended into the shading of the hat. Several of these demons had red eyes that almost glowed in the shadowy light rising from the floor beneath the painting. She glanced back at the demons that made up the face. Yes. There. And there. Demons with red eyes that seemed to glow. If she stood back, would that red glow look like pimples?

Strange thought, but normal enough to keep her from falling into the well of horror within the painting.

Every closer look, she picked up more detail. All the background, that melting landscape that, from a few feet away, looked like a blurry, indistinct city park, was filled with cavorting demons. And now she saw all the things the demons were cavorting around. Humans in various stages of torture, on pikes, over spits, the demons tearing into them, raping and eating and gutting and skinning and…

She swallowed hard and pulled back from the picture to take a deep breath. A mistake, though, because she stood closer to the victim here, and the smell of blood was stronger. It coated her tongue. She didn't look at down at Melissa James. She couldn't just then.

How the hell was this woman able to draw this portrait? Had *wanted* to specifically draw this piece?

Maybe she'd just wanted to draw the overview, without all the creepy little details. Anne walked to the fallen sketchbook and looked closer at the pictures she could see without touching the book or flipping pages. The top one, the one ripped, was a full-page sketch of the portrait, the outline of the man, no details from the background yet, some shading in the face and clothing.

She squatted down to get a better look at the ripped picture. It was torn across the face of the portrait, so the part with the single eye visible to viewers was gone. But on the page under the ripped one was another image that had the eye in detail, drawn larger than in the original portrait. Inside the eye…a lot of little dancing demons. The pupil was a single demon staring out of the picture, its mouth opened wide in a teeth-revealing grin and a forked tongue winding from its mouth. Melissa had gotten the detail so precise it looked like the tongue was literally lifting out of the page.

Anne shook her head and stood, glancing back at the portrait. She'd missed the eye detail completely. Did she dare see that evil looking little demon in the original? Maybe in a minute. Right now, she was creeped out enough by the black and white sketch of it.

But obviously, Melissa had intended on drawing the portrait with all the demon details.

Still standing, Anne glanced at the other pages she could see in the sketchbook, the ones flipping around in the gallery's softly heated air. There were some more smaller studies of the eye, different specific parts of the image, some preliminary studies of the background details. She glanced at the large eye study visible through the rip again. That sketch made the little demon so much larger, she could see it even at a distance.

Distance did not help make it any less horrifying.

The exhibitions "grotesque and cursed" name lived up to its art. But also, unfortunately for Melissa, lived up to reality. Anne briefly glanced back at the dead woman. Suarez had told her, at the first and only other murder scene she'd worked, that it was easier sometimes to see the victim as "victim" than by their name.

Anne just saw Melissa.

She took a deep breath, squeezing her nostrils together so she wouldn't pull in too much of the blood smell.

"Ready?" Suarez asked quietly.

"No." She stepped as close to the body as she dared, staying out of the blood pool. "Forensics has gotten everything right?"

"Trace, yes. Pictures as well." He gestured at the sketchbook and pencils. "Obviously they have to finish, so be careful. But you're cleared to touch the body."

"What about the portrait?"

"The…portrait? You want to touch that?"

"Want is not the right word. But yes, I think I might need to."

She glanced up in time to see him open his mouth, snap it closed again. His expression pinched, a look she knew meant he was thinking.

She'd worked with Suarez more when he'd been in the fraud division. Since his move to homicide, she had only worked with him that one other time. She wondered if he was still finding his place in his new job or if he felt comfortable with his skills. And what did that feel like? Being comfortable with one's skills?

He ran a hand through his shortly cropped dark hair and blew out a breath. "The museum director has asked us to be careful about the art and not touch anything we didn't need to." He nodded at the creepy portrait. "She was very specific that we not touch that picture in particular. Said it's worth a few million."

If Anne had been the kind of person to gasp, she would have gasped then. She settled for raised brows. "Millions?"

She glanced at the creepy portrait. The artist had obviously been of considerable skill to make it work. And it was a pretty impressive piece when taken objectively. But it was so supremely disturbing, someone would have to pay *her* to be anywhere near it. Which, in point of fact, was what was happening. She wouldn't have chosen to be in the same room with that piece if the NYPD weren't paying her to be here.

She didn't really even want to touch the thing. A very large part of her hoped she wouldn't have to. Even at a distance now, she could see the little demons making up the details of the man's face and hat. If she stared at the eye, she saw the demon Melissa had taken such care to detail in her sketches. Anne turned away, breaking the stare, but the hairs on her neck stood up, and she had to will herself not to look back. The sense of something looking at her, of being watched, was strong enough to make her shiver.

"You cold? You need your coat?" Suarez asked.

She'd left it outside the gallery with the rest of the team when she'd donned the protective coverings that would keep her from tracking anything into the murder scene. "No. I'm good." The gallery was warm enough. And she didn't want her coat in here anyway. It might pick up the smell.

The scent of blood seemed to grow stronger, even as she thought about it, so she stopped thinking about smells and turned her attention back to Melissa. "Can you ask the director about me touching the portrait? I'd like permission before I get started, so I don't have to stop midway and wait."

"Sure. Sure." Suarez gave her a little look. "You okay in here until I get back?"

She nodded at the two other officers in the gallery, keeping their distance, but still watching the proceedings. "I'll be fine."

She glanced at the portrait from the corner of her eye.

Probably she'd be fine.

CHAPTER TWO

ith Suarez gone, Anne took a few steps away from the body and squatted down again, taking in Melissa's position on the floor, the way her pencils and sketchbook had been scattered. "Did forensics collect the ripped part of the portrait?" she asked the cops hovering at the edge of the room.

"Wasn't found," one cop said, her voice quiet.

Anne didn't know either of these officers, so she couldn't really judge their moods. But the cop sounded tense. Anne couldn't blame her.

"The part that was ripped away is missing?"

"Wasn't found in here," the cop repeated.

Anne nodded, her gaze still on Melissa, though she actively tried to avoid looking at all the blood. She wasn't squeamish, except when it came to mice, rats, and cockroaches—hazards of living in the city—but there seemed to be an awful lot of blood for one woman. Not looking at it while still looking at Melissa's face took a lot of effort.

She glanced back at the ripped picture, then up at the portrait. This time, the details seemed even clearer, the little demons and the torture much more evident, even at a distance. Once you saw it, you couldn't unsee it? Probably. She would have preferred unseeing it, though.

She couldn't imagine *wanting* to recreate this portrait, coming here specifically to practice on this piece. Especially not the details. Back in the day, if someone had wanted her to create a forgery of this painting, she'd have turned down the job. Spending that much time with the thing… The idea of it made her shiver again, despite the warm air.

Maybe it was the warm air that was making the scent of blood stronger. Overpowering the scent of lemon cleaner and whatever the incense had been. There seemed to be…more to it now, too. Not just blood scent, but other things… Things that reminded her of burnt meat.

If someone was standing outside this room eating a hamburger, she was going to ralph.

A noise behind her had her standing and spinning to face the gallery's main doors, which had been closed to keep people out of the crime scene. A woman in clicking heals and a pencil sharp black skirt suit came storming into the gallery. The two police officers in the room moved to block her way so she couldn't come in any farther. She pointed past them at Anne.

"You cannot touch, move, or in any way damage any of the paintings in here," she said. "Do you understand how valuable these pieces are? Someone without training cannot be permitted to touch them."

"I have training," Anne said. "Twelve years at the Met working in the fine arts galleries. Five years before that at the Orsay." These were true credentials as far as they went. Leaving out some of the finer details of those fifteen years. The museum director didn't need to know everything.

Dr. Tameryn Gilbert, director of the Museum of Small

Art, was the sort of woman often called handsome instead of pretty. Tall, thin, with a short bob of black hair and sharp features that lent themselves to smug eyebrow raises—which probably worked in her favor in her job. Minimal jewelry, expertly dramatic makeup, red lipstick that popped against her pale skin. When she pursed her lips, that red formed a remarkably perfect heart shape.

Anne pulled a pair of white gloves from the pocket of her protective jumpsuit. "I'll use these if it will make you happier." Gloves didn't interfere with her psychic readings, which was both a boon and a complication, depending on the circumstances. "I have no intention of moving the piece. I'm going to touch the canvas briefly, with just my fingertips, and then I'll be done."

"No. You don't understand. You can't." Dr. Gilbert looked at the cops blocking her way, frustration deepening creases on her brow.

"Why can't I?" Anne asked. Curious, not defensive. "I promise I have experience with delicate artwork. I won't damage it."

She hadn't been told anything specific about the pieces in the exhibit or their value, until Suarez mentioned the value of the demon filled portrait a few minutes ago. No histories, no details of the artists, not even the age of the pieces. Detective Suarez thought it gave her analysis more legitimacy when she didn't know many background facts. At least with his superiors. So she humored him. So long as the department paid her, she usually didn't care if they believed her or not. At least not for the fraud and theft cases. The murder cases… She cared about those a little more.

But the director seemed more desperate to stop her touching the portrait than Anne would have expected. Especially after hearing Anne's credentials. Dr. Gilbert twisted her hands together, glancing from Anne, to the portrait, to the cops. The nervous gesture looked awkward and wrong on the woman, though Anne wasn't sure why. She'd just gotten the impression Dr. Gilbert wasn't the fidgeting type.

She was fidgeting now.

Detective Suarez had come into the room behind the director moments after she stormed into the gallery, but he hung back, his own expression neutral and impossible to read, his attention focused on the director.

"It's…" Dr. Gilbert started, then pressed her lips together and glanced at the painting. "You see, it's…the sort of piece that has to be handled very…very delicately."

Anne raised her white gloves again. "Which is why I brought these."

"No. No, you don't understand."

"Enlighten me."

"It's…" She glanced at the cops still blocking her path. "It's cursed, all right."

Anne's gaze jumped to Suarez to see how he'd react to that. His neutral expression didn't change. Had he been told this before or was this news to him? "What sort of curse?" she asked the director.

"The bad sort of curse," Dr. Gilbert spat.

"Like King Tut?" one of the cops said, his tone snarky and disbelieving.

His partner elbowed him. "Don't disrespect curses," she hissed. "You don't want to bring that shit down on you."

"The officer isn't far off," Dr. Gilbert said, though she was speaking to Anne. "Like the Tutankhamun curse, this curse has a long history and has, according to the stories, claimed a few lives."

Anne raised her brows but resisted glancing back at Melissa's body.

The director winced. "I didn't think… She was just sketching it. She's here a lot. I trusted her not to touch anything. She's a very… Was a very good artist. I wanted to encourage her. I didn't think sketching the piece would… harm her."

"How did she get in here after hours? Did you let her stay after closing?"

"No. That's the thing… She left when we locked up yesterday. She walked out with one of our regular volunteers, Beatrice. They were talking about going for a drink. I was shocked to find Melissa here this morning."

Probably shocked in several distinct ways. Anne looked at Suarez. "Volunteer."

He nodded and stepped out of the room.

"The Tutankhamun curse was later proven just a story," Anne said, keeping the director focused on her. "The deaths traced to mold inside the tomb. Is it possible the deaths associated with the portrait are similarly coincidental or have more mundane explanations?"

Not that she discounted the effects of curses—she was a witch after all—but in her experience, the real power of a curse was the belief in it more than any actual magic. The story, the myth of it, the belief, was usually all a curse needed to work.

"*The Everyman's Soul* curse is…" The director swallowed. "I hesitated to allow the piece here. I'm well aware of its history, the rumors. But I thought… We'll be careful. It's one of many pieces. I'm sure the curse is just a story to raise its price. It's a well-crafted painting but its monetary value would likely be less impressive if not for the curse."

Anne agreed with the director's assessment of the painting's value. It was called *The Everyman's Soul*? Interesting name. Anne started to glance back at it, but resisted the urge. She wanted to keep the director talking. She also wanted to get her part of this investigation done so she could go home and shower and rinse the scent of blood from her nose. And that strange scent of burning meat. That one was really starting to get to her, because she couldn't pinpoint the source.

"How did you get it into position? You're insistent I don't touch it. Someone had to touch it to hang it on the wall."

"Two of the security staff that travel with the exhibition positioned the piece for us. My assistant oversaw the placement. But none of my people touched it."

"You're sure?"

Again, she was mostly just curious. Curses were all well and good, but Melissa hadn't died of some mysterious illness. She'd been murdered and left in a pool of blood. Suarez hadn't told her *how* Melissa had been murdered yet—it wasn't obvious at a glance where the blood was coming from or how it had been forced from Melissa's body. Like the history of the various art pieces, Suarez wanted her coming to the body with as little information as possible to ensure her reading was "clean," in his words. But it was obviously a violent death and not a wasting, mold-related illness. Unless *The Everyman* had stepped out of the portrait to kill Melissa, this had all the hallmarks of a real human murderer.

The question was, did the murderer know about the curse? And if so, was the curse part of the plan?

"No one touched the portrait," Dr. Gilbert insisted. "Everyone who works here, volunteers and staff, understood the restrictions. For the most part, only my assistant had anything to do with this exhibit anyway. Most of the regular docents refused to stay in this room."

"Your assistant spent a lot time in here?"

"Ms. Zoric is a particular fan of this exhibition. She's the one who lobbied to have us host it here."

"She likes demonic art?"

"Gothic art. Yes. It's her specialty."

Gothic was a good word for some of the things in the exhibit. But when Anne thought of Gothic, she thought of giant churches in Europe with elaborate gargoyle statuary. *The Everyman's Soul* portrait...

Gothic seemed too tame a word for it.

CHAPTER THREE

efore Anne could ask the director any more questions, Detective Suarez returned to the gallery room with a young woman Anne assumed to be the volunteer. She was mid-twenties, probably close to Melissa's age, and dressed in comfortable dress slacks, a long-sleeved blouse, and low heels. Her makeup streaked down her light brown cheeks, and when she glanced in the direction of Melissa's body, she started crying again.

Anne made a move to stand between the young woman and the body, though it wouldn't really hide anything.

"It's all my fault," the woman stuttered through her tears. "I told her no one would mind. I encouraged her."

"Beatrice? What are you saying?" Dr. Gilbert turned on the young woman.

"We…we met Oxana at the bar," Beatrice said, sniffing.

Suarez handed her a tissue from a small pack he'd had in his suit jacket pocket. Anne hadn't realized he carried those.

"Melissa showed her some of the sketches she'd done so far," Beatrice continued after blowing her nose. "They were so good! She'd gotten the details down really well. I can't stand this exhibition, but there was no doubt Melissa had really captured the essence of the piece, you know?"

Beatrice glanced at Dr. Gilbert, keeping her body turned away from Melissa.

"Oxana?" Anne asked, frowning a little at Suarez.

"My assistant, Oxana Zoric," Dr. Gilbert said.

Anne nodded and motioned Beatrice to continue.

Beatrice looked between the director and the cops. "I didn't want to say anything. Didn't want anyone to get in trouble." She dabbed her nose with the tissue again, gulping in air. "Oxana said she could get Melissa back into the gallery if she wanted to work on her sketches in peace, without all the people walking around. Melissa was hesitant." Beatrice glanced at Dr. Gilbert again. "She didn't want to get Oxana in trouble or risk being banned from the museum if she was caught. I...I encouraged her." She raised her hands, a pleading motion. "She'd been talking about that damned painting *all* night. She was obsessed, and I thought if she got a chance to finally finish, she'd be able to let it go. I thought... I thought one night of drawing and she'd be done with it. I didn't know. How could I know?"

"Know what?" Anne asked.

"The curse," Beatrice wailed. "No one told me about the curse."

Beatrice turned her tear-streaked face into Suarez's shoulder, which seemed to startle him. He gave the young woman an awkward pat on the back and looked at the other cops with a kind of panicked expression that might have been funny under different circumstances. One of the cops moved from in front of Dr. Gilbert to take Beatrice into a secure hold. Suarez gave a nod and the cop walked Beatrice back out of the gallery, letting her lean on him.

Anne held Suarez's gaze for a long moment. "Ms. Zoric is outside?" she asked.

"She is. One of the officers is taking her statement. She hasn't said anything about coming back here after closing."

"Of course she wouldn't," Dr. Gilbert said, her brows lowered, her mouth set in a tight line. "I'd fire her for that. Letting someone into the museum after hours and leaving her unsupervised with all this art?"

"Where was the security team during all this?" Anne asked. "The ones who travel with the exhibition?"

Dr. Gilbert blinked. "They… They should have been here." She looked around as if looking for one of the guards. "We have security systems in place, but at least one member of the exhibition's security team stays inside the museum overnight. It's a requirement of the insurance policy."

"Was there anyone here when you arrived this morning?"

"Now that you mention it? No. No, there wasn't. That's…" Dr. Gilbert looked away, frowning.

Suarez gave Anne a nod and ducked out of the gallery again.

Dr. Gilbert looked between Anne and the spot where Suarez had been. Then she sighed. "Why do you want to touch the painting?"

The cop still keeping Dr. Gilbert from walking farther into the gallery didn't turn around, but Anne saw her head tilt just a little. Suarez didn't tell anyone but his chief the specific reason he brought Anne in to cases. Most assumed it was her art knowledge because every case Suarez brought her in on had something to do with art—even the two murders. According to Suarez, cops could be superstitious and if they knew she was a witch and a psychic, they might get weird.

To be fair, the witch part was just theological. She didn't have any real magic to speak of. But the psychic part was one of her gifts, right along with a keen ability to recreate exactly any painting she stared at for more than two minutes. The two gifts were linked, her psychic abilities tied into her eye for art details. She wasn't sure why. She hadn't really tried to figure it out. Both skills had helped her in her past career. And they were helping her establish this new, less illegal one now.

But she was fine with the cops assuming she was here for her art expertise. She didn't want to deal with superstitious misunderstandings and myths about her religion either.

So her answer to Dr. Gilbert was a half-truth, a hedging. "I will lean in very close to look for any trace evidence the forensic team missed. My expertise allows me to see things that might be…lost in the paint by an inexpert eye." So to speak.

Dr. Gilbert frowned. "I can tell you if there's any…" She swallowed hard and very deliberately didn't look at Melissa's body. "Any evidence without having to touch the portrait."

"No unauthorized people are allowed near the crime scene," the remaining cop said. "We can't allow you close enough to look at the painting in detail."

Thank you, officer. Anne should probably get her name before she left. Knowing the cops that helped rather than hindered, and could hold it together in the face of a bloody murder scene, seemed useful.

Though, frankly, she hoped she wouldn't be around many more dead bodies in the future. She sort of wished Suarez hadn't taken that promotion to homicide.

For absolutely no reason she could fathom, the smell of blood and burnt meat got stronger. She wrinkled her nose. Wow, she needed to get this over with soon. She had to get out of this room before that smell got any worse.

She was a little surprised to see Dr. Gilbert frown and reach up to delicately cover her nose. The police officer was keeping her well away from the scene, and the air circulation in the gallery was excellent, the air filters working overtime to ensure the art was protected. The smell must really be getting stronger if it traveled that far across the room.

Dr. Gilbert let out a sigh from behind her hand and said, "If you must. But please, please, don't touch it if you don't have to. I don't put a lot of stock into curses, not really, but…" She glanced in the opposite direction of Melissa's body, the gesture telling.

Anne carefully stepped around Melissa and the fallen pencils and sketchbook again, moving as close to the portrait as she dared get. Slipping on her gloves, she studied the image again. Now the dancing demons were so obvious the "face" of the man no longer made much sense. Her eye couldn't pick it out anymore. All she saw when she looked at the image was a writhing mass of pale demons and dark demons with scattered touches of red. She blinked a few times, trying to resee the image of the man's profile, but failed. Even the eye just looked like a demon climbing out of a circular window now. A demon that looked directly at her, smiling its teeth-revealing, malevolent grin.

She didn't want to touch the portrait any more than Dr. Gilbert wanted her to. Not for the same reasons, though. She didn't want to see what it had to tell her. She stared at the demon in the eye for a long moment, and considered if maybe she should start with Melissa's body. She was more likely to get details there than from the portrait. But the painting drew her even as it repulsed her. Stretching her hand forward, she leaned in very close to the image—a show for the director— and let her fingers hover over the center of the canvas as she braced herself.

"No! Stop!"

CHAPTER FOUR

The shout had Anne startling upright and spinning around to face the source of the abrupt command. But putting her back to the demon-filled portrait overwhelmed her with an unexpectedly primal terror. She moved to one side, taking comfort in having a plain brick wall behind her.

The woman at the entrance lurched against Suarez's hold, trying harder than the director had to get into the gallery. She was a lot smaller than Suarez, barely five foot, and her blond hair was swept up into the kind of elaborate, smooth twist Anne associated with socialites. She was dressed in a dark skirt suit similar to the director's, but she was curvier, so the suit looked less severe. She was older than Beatrice. Maybe in her early forties. Maybe a little older. But obviously working to fend off signs of aging with makeup and, if Anne guessed right, a little filler here and there.

"Don't touch that," she hissed, struggling against Suarez's hold. "Don't you dare."

"The director has given me permission," Anne said.

"No! She doesn't know. She doesn't understand. No one does. He does. He knows." She struggled harder. "You can't!"

Anne frowned. "You're going to have to explain that. He who?" Maybe the security guard who should have been here last night?

"Him." The woman pointed to the portrait.

Anne didn't shiver. But she wanted to.

"What does he know?" Suarez asked, his tone quiet and gentle. His expression was impossible to read, but there was a very soothing note in his voice.

The woman wasn't soothed. "You can't touch him. He's mine. No one can have him. He's mine!"

Well. That was…a lot. "You want the portrait?" Anne asked.

"Ms. Zoric, what are you talking about?" Dr. Gilbert said, confirming the woman as her assistant.

"He's calling me," Oxana said, still jerking against Suarez's hold. "He knows you mean him harm."

Whoa. Okay. "That's an oil painting," Anne said, slowly, calmly. "It can't call you. You know that right?"

"He belongs to me. I belong to him. We're bonded, you see? I'm the only one allowed to touch him. Only me! She broke that rule. She was warned. I warned her. Don't touch him. Draw him. Honor him. But *don't* touch him."

Anne didn't glance down at Melissa, but she saw Suarez's mouth compress.

Dr. Gilbert's eyes widened and she dropped her hand from over her nose. "Oxana, what have you done?"

"What I had to. I had to. He told me. No one is supposed to touch him but me."

"Who told you that, Oxana?" Anne asked. "The security guard who was supposed to be here?"

Oxana laughed, and it wasn't a pleasant sound. "He tried

to stop me. Tried to stop us, prevent us from being together, prevent her from honoring his glory."

Oh oh. Anne had an awful feeling there was another body around here somewhere. She saw the same realization in Suarez's eyes when he looked at her.

Suarez nodded at the last remaining cop. She left with a backward glance at the portrait, her jaw tight as she hurried from the gallery.

"What have you done, Oxana?" Dr. Gilbert asked again. "Whatever it is, we can help you. I'll make sure you get help. Lawyers. Whatever you need." She was looking frantically between Anne and Suarez and Oxana, as if she wasn't sure what to do or what to think.

"I don't need lawyers," Oxana said with a snarl. "I just need him."

She launched forward again, so suddenly she managed to jerk free of Suarez's hold. He cursed violently and lunged for the smaller woman, but she was already halfway across the gallery.

Anne didn't really think about what she was doing. Not distinctly. She might later say she was worried Oxana would trample evidence around the body. Or she was afraid Oxana would damage the portrait. But really, in the moment, she reacted without thinking.

She pushed away from the wall, raced forward, and planted herself between Oxana and the portrait. The woman was smaller, but determined. And she had momentum behind her. So the force of the impact rocked Anne back on her heals. She grabbed onto Oxana to both restrain her and hold onto her own balance.

And the images poured in.

A knife, elaborate, silver. A gift from him. Found inside one of the statues. No one else knew about it. Only him. He'd told her. Plunging into the artist's back. Again. And again. And again. She'd dared touch him. She touched him! She was warned not to. Not allowed. He'd said so. He'd told her exactly what to do. Kill the man, too. Yes. Kill the man. He tried to stop her. No one could stop her. Not with him by her side. He loved her. He would always love her.

Anne jerked out of the vision and pulled away from Oxana the minute Suarez had hold of her again. Anne blinked hard, folding over and putting her hands on her knees as she gulped in air.

She'd allowed herself to "see" into a lot of people over the years. She'd survived in her former line of work by being able to read the people who employed her and avoid the ones who might double cross her or try to cheat her out of her, substantial, fee. She'd even encountered two different killers.

But never one so…unmoored. The other two had been cold. Calculating. Vicious. But not out of control.

Oxana was out of control.

"The curse," Dr. Gilbert whispered from across the galley. Her voice carried surprisingly well in the otherwise heavy silence.

CHAPTER FIVE

nne didn't straighten because she was still blinking back spots from her vision, her hands braced on her knees so she didn't fall down, her head bent toward the floor so she could concentrate on breathing. But she did manage to tell Suarez, "Your people are going to want to open up the bottom of that statue in the corner. The dancing satyr with the flute. There's a knife in the base. That'll be the murder weapon."

"No! You can't keep us apart. You can't!" Oxana jerked against Suarez's hands, but he held her firmly now.

"You okay?" Suarez asked Anne.

She waved him off. "Be fine in a minute. Go do what you have to do."

He walked a screaming, protesting Oxana from the room, leaving the sounds of her shouts echoing in the large gallery. The scent of blood and burnt meat clogged Anne's nose, coated her tongue. She had to get out of this room.

She hurried out, following Dr. Gilbert who followed Suarez and Oxana. Anne took off the protective jumpsuit and booties, retrieved her coat and purse from the cop who'd been watching her stuff for her, and went outside to sit on the sidewalk in front of the museum.

The traffic from Houston Street rumbled loudly in the background, as people trod past, not even giving her a glance as she leaned against the smooth stone wall of the Museum of Small Art, trying to clear her nostrils in the sharp cold air, grateful for the ordinary city smells, the warm cars and tarmac, the roasting nuts from the food cart at the corner, the pizza place across the street. Somehow, the fact that it was bright and sunny out felt strangely disconnected from what had happened inside.

"You okay?"

Anne looked up, shading her eyes, to see one of the police officers from inside the gallery. The one who'd known to be careful of curses. Anne smiled at her. "Fine. Clearing my head a little."

"Not every day you see a dead body."

"Nope," she confirmed.

The officer shuffled from one foot to the other, her gaze skimming over the street. "Thought you might want to know we found the security guard. He was…" She made a vague hand gesture. "Probably wouldn't have found his body in that closet for a day or more. The director said it wasn't a part of the museum used much."

Something Oxana would have known. "Thanks for telling me."

"We found the knife, too. In the statue. Along with the ripped page from the sketchbook." She made a face. "Was the part of the picture that had the eye." She shivered. "Anyway." She hesitated. "Thought you should know."

"Thanks, Officer…?"

"Mitchell."

"Thanks, Officer Mitchell. I appreciate the update."

"You believe in curses, Ms. Reynolds?"

"I do," she said.

"You think that picture is cursed?"

"No idea. Glad I didn't need to touch it in the end."

Mitchell snorted. "You need anything?"

"I'm good. Thanks again."

Mitchell tipped her hat and went back into the museum, her gaze still skimming over the street and the passing pedestrians.

The cold from sitting on the sidewalk had started to creep through the seat of Anne's jeans by the time Suarez came outside. He sat next to her without hesitating.

"You're going to mess up your suit," she said, her attention remaining firmly on the street.

"That's what dry cleaning is for." He kept his gaze on the street as well, leaning back against the building with her as they watched people coming in and out of the pizza restaurant across the street. After a few minutes, he said, "Officer Mitchell told you we found the knife and the other body?"

"Yup."

"Glad you didn't have to touch that portrait."

"I said the same to Officer Mitchell."

"I have a lot of paperwork and reports and things to finish, but… You need a drink?"

"I don't drink."

"Not even water? Don't you get dehydrated?"

She smiled without looking at him. "Cranberry juice and Sprite might help."

"Meet you at the station," he said. "After the paperwork and we file your payment request, we'll head out to Walters. Think we're all gonna need a drink."

"You believe in curses, Suarez?"

"Nope." He stood. "But I'm open to change." He gave her a little half solute and went back inside the museum.

Anne blinked, the image of the demon climbing out of the portrait's eye hovering, ready to find its way into her nightmares. She pushed herself up off the sidewalk and headed for the subway that would take her to the police station. Paperwork first. Drink next.

Figure out how to sleep later.

But that was one painting she had no intention of duplicating. There just wasn't enough money in the world.

One *Everyman's Soul* was enough.

DEMONIC DATES

CHAPTER ONE

*L*exie Alexander stared at the invitation in her hand, the expensive cream card, the gold leafing, the faint fragrance of musk that emerged with the square of paper whenever she pulled it from its envelope. An envelope that had been sealed with wax and pressed with a single initial.

Then she looked up at the house. Alone on a hill, outside the borders of the nearest town, but not so far away as to make the journey to town a day long event. Surrounded by a forest of maple and oak, an earthy loam mingling with the faint musk of the invitation. The house itself was what her grandmother would have politely called…interesting.

Which was maybe an understatement.

Three stories, at least above ground. And a strange mix of Victorian peaks and porches, with a castle-like stone wing to one side and an almost New York Brownstone look to the other. A large, square of a building with all these different elements sprouting off in different directions. Everything about the arrangement looked wrong. An assault on the eyes.

Like the architect had been on LSD when they'd designed the place and just tacked on whatever took their fancy.

It wasn't a pretty house either. Not even a little. Despite the lovely finial designs decorating the tops of the gables on the more Victorian parts of the roof, and the almost comically fun gargoyles spitting on the castle side, and the sweeping stairs leading up to a large oak door on the Brownstone side. None of it...went together. There was no flow or cohesion. Not even the colors worked together. A dark gray with bright purple highlights in the Victorian parts, gray stonework in the castle with no break for color, and a soft muted orange on the Brownstone walls, with some white decorative elements.

Staring at the house was disorienting. Made Lexie feel like she was falling forward even though she wasn't moving. Like if she took a step toward the house, the ground would suddenly vanish, and she'd fall on her face. Or worse, just keep falling into some kind of abyss.

The temptation to turn around, return to her car, drive back down the hill, and ignore the invitation was strong. Stronger than she'd have expected given how excited she'd been to receive the invitation in the first place.

Not every witch gets the opportunity to visit the home of one of the most notorious witches in the history of witches. The witch who'd tried to loose a hoard of demons on the fanatics who were burning witches in the seventeenth century here in the US. She'd been destroyed by her own coven in the end, because she refused to stop letting demons into this realm, and those demons weren't restricting their havoc to fanatical witch-burners.

Her name was never spoken. Not many witches even knew of her. In fact, most didn't from what Lexie had learned. Only a very few, a tiny handful over the last few centuries, kept the knowledge as a warning, a lesson from history to be avoided. Lexie had learned of the infamous witch through her own grandmother, who'd passed the knowledge down from her grandmother. Lexie was charged now with keeping that history.

The house wasn't the exact place the witch had lived of course. It had been added to over the years. But the core of it was her home. Somewhere in the middle of all that chaotic architectural junk was the place this witch had lived, learned, tested her magic, and plotted her revenge.

And because Lexie was a historical record keeper, a collector of details to record and preserve, even if the information was too dangerous to release to most, she couldn't have resisted an invitation to this particular place if she'd tried. Especially given the date.

The invitation coming from said witch's very mysterious and enigmatic ancestor was even more irresistible. There were rumors about him, some of which she'd decided had to be more myth than reality, some of which had made her… wonder. But all of it had her curious. Extremely curious.

Which, as her grandmother would say, was the trait that killed the cat.

But she wasn't a cat. She was a historian. A record keeper for the witchy community. And this was a bit of history that, even if she couldn't share it wide, should be preserved.

Or at least that's what she'd told herself when she'd rented a car and driven up here from New York, to a house located miles outside of modern-day Salem, Massachusetts.

She'd studied the location on various map apps and had assured herself the place wasn't *that* isolated. The main road got plenty of traffic, and she could still hear that in the distance. There were some scattered farms and houses in the area, though the closest was a mile away. But really, that wasn't *that* far.

A cold autumn breeze lifted her hair off her neck, sending a chill down her spine, despite her heavy wool coat. This late in the season, almost November, and the winter cold was already creeping in, portending things to come. She didn't mind. Lexie liked all the seasons. But the breeze, in just that moment, felt like the dance of cold cold fingers along her spine.

A warning and a threat.

She huffed out an irritated breath with herself. Then she, metaphorically, pulled up her big girl pants, straightened the strap of her oversized purse on her shoulder, and marched up to what she hoped was the front door. She was here to do some research. On a historically important witch. Whose ancestor had sent her a special invitation to come to the house and do that research on this historically important date. There was nothing to fear and no reason to run.

It was just a fucking house after all.

MILES REID WATCHED AS THE WOMAN APPROACHED THE house with trepidation. He couldn't blame her. This wasn't the sort of house people approached without trepidation even if they didn't know the history of the original occupant.

And even if they did know who the original occupant had been, that part of the house was barely visible around the construction that had gone on in the following centuries. Construction designed to cover up, hide, obscure the past.

And still demons lurked in these walls.

He'd inherited the monstrosity from a cousin, who'd inherited it from another branch of the family, who'd quickly tossed it into his branch of the family at their earliest convenience. The original occupant hadn't had children, so the house had always been passed to a non-direct line from her, but it had almost become like a game of hot potato or keep away. Tossing the house quickly to the next owner so the bad stuff didn't rub off.

When Miles had inherited, it had very much felt like his cousin had said, "Tag! You're it." And run away very fast.

Now Miles was stuck with this place.

They couldn't bulldoze it—many a relative had been tempted—because the *house* resisted that. The bulldozers came out, and things went wrong. Engines broke. Tires went flat. Important bits fell off. He didn't know a lot about bulldozers—he was a journalist and not a construction worker —but two owners ago, a clever cousin did actually try to raze the place, and the stories of the disasters that befell that attempt were family legends.

Despite those legends. He was still tempted to have the place knocked. Just all of it, flattened and buried over and wiped from the world.

But first, he had to figure out what it was about the *house* that stopped all efforts to do anything but add more weird architecture around it. Why did the place insist on existing? If he could figure that out, he could figure out a way to get rid of it.

Or at the very least, make it less dangerous.

Which was why he'd sent the fancy invitation to Lexie Alexander, witch historian. He'd had to research for more than six months to find her. While a lot of Wiccans and other neo-pagans were out and open about their religion, finding a real witch who knew about the real history of his distant ancestor proved complicated. A lot of the witches he'd met and interviewed hadn't even heard of her.

There was probably a reason for that.

Her name wasn't spoken in his family. She was referred

to euphemistically. And the branch of the family that had shared her last name had died off about a hundred years ago, which made it easier not to say her name. If they didn't talk about her directly within her own family, it was entirely possible those outside his family had purposefully erased her from history, too. He wasn't sure *why*, because again, no one in his family spoke about it. But whatever that original witch had done, it had been bad.

When Miles had finally discovered the existence of an actual witch historian, a sort of record keeper for the history of witches in this country, he'd been sure he'd found the right person to help. He'd very nearly just sent off an email and invited her to the house.

And then, for some reason, he hadn't. He still wasn't entirely sure why he'd had the fancy invitation card made. Some…impulse he went with because it felt right. Maybe he thought she'd need to be intrigued or else she wouldn't knock on the door? Maybe he'd worried she'd think he was crazy if he just asked her outright? Whatever the reasoning, sending out the fancy invitation with the actual name of his ancestor in it felt…appropriate. So he'd done it.

Then felt like a fool for a week afterward. He was certain she'd think it was some kind of joke and ignore it, and he'd have to send a ridiculous email explaining why he'd sent the invitation in the first place—even though he had no idea— and she'd probably still think this was a scam of some kind. And he wouldn't even be able to blame her.

Seeing her here, walking cautiously up to the front door, was such a relief it made his chest ache. Maybe now *now* he could get some answers and find a way to divest his family of this damned house. This…curse.

He studied her as she studied the front door. She was average height, maybe a little taller, but not tall. Light brown hair—in the bright autumn sun she'd had streaks of blond and red in it—brushing her shoulders, eyes a color he couldn't see from the distance, pale skin, sharp features. Pretty. Not glamorous or head turning, but pleasant to look at. She was dressed for the cooler weather in jeans and a light wool jacket, a thin scarf wrapped around her neck. She kept looking down at the invitation in her hand and then up at the door, like she might bolt at any moment.

Miles was trying to be patient and let her ring the doorbell, or knock. If he flung the door open now, too eagerly to have her inside, she'd definitely run away. He was a little afraid his desperation for answers was going to be too obvious as it was, and he couldn't afford to scare her off. So he waited, tapping his foot, discreetly watching her from a bay window in the Victorian wing that gave a good angle on the front porch, and hoping she knocked before she spotted him. If she caught him watching her like this, he could only imagine what she'd think.

So he probably should stop watching her, he thought. But waiting for her to knock without knowing what she was doing —or if she'd turned around and left—would be worse. His nerves couldn't take it.

He needed answers. And it was entirely possible Lexie Alexander was the only person who could give him those answers.

Without her help, he'd be stuck with this house, this pit of… He hesitated to call it evil, though he frequently got that sense. But he'd seen real evil in the world before. This felt too amorphous and vague to call it evil before he figured out what *it* was. He just knew whatever *it* was, it was not good.

And he wanted away from it. He wanted out of this house, wanted the burden of it gone from his life—without having to die to achieve that. The cousin he'd inherited from had died of cancer, and he'd never seen a man so happy to die of cancer than Jim had been, when he'd informed Miles the house was about to be his. Miles really didn't want that same fate. So he'd done what he did best and researched the problem.

Lexie Alexander was his answer.

Finally, finally she put a careful finger to the doorbell button and pushed.

CHAPTER TWO

exie pressed her lips together so she didn't gasp when the door flew open. She'd half expected it to creek on noisy hinges to match the rest of the overwhelmingly odd house. Instead, the door opened easily, noiselessly, and onto the face of a man she…wasn't expecting either.

Handsome. That was her first thought. Why hadn't she expected that Miles Reid might be handsome? Honestly, she hadn't given his appearance more than a cursory thought. And that cursory thought had inserted something significantly older, darker, more intense, and less…vital. Yes, vital was the right word.

He wasn't particularly tall, but a few inches taller than her. Short dark hair and a nice color brown for his eyes, a good face, not hard or calculating or cold. In fact, he rather radiated earnestness. And maybe a little desperation, which he was trying to hide. The way he stuffed his hands into his jeans pockets and rocked back on his heels, the slight tension around his otherwise attractive smile were tells.

Nervous around a witch? Or nervous about the house?

She was nervous about the house. And she didn't know enough about him yet to know if he believed in *real* witches. Even if he owned the former home of a notorious one. What did he know about his ancestor? How much did he know?

The rumors of him, claiming him mysterious and maybe even dangerous seemed unlikely now, as she stared at him. He appeared too…well, ordinary. Handsome but ordinary. Her instincts weren't screaming at her to be leery or to be careful of *him*. The house… That was another story. Her instincts, now that she was standing on the porch, were sending her all kinds of warnings about the house.

She was going to be the heroine in the movie that was too stupid to live and walk into that house, but thanks to her nagging instincts, she was aware she was doing the stupid thing.

But Miles Reid wasn't invoking any of those cautious and leery reactions. He looked as nervous and uncertain as she felt, and that was calming.

Though she had a hard time reconciling the man in front of her with the elaborate invitation she'd been sent to tour the house. That invitation belonged to the mysterious man of rumor, a man wearing all black, with hard features and a shadowed existence in the dark.

Miles was a white man, and a little pale, but there was enough color in his cheeks to prove he left the house in the daylight. Broad shouldered, maybe a bit extra around the middle. And his button-down shirt was a light blue. Nothing he wore screamed scary, intimidating stranger. He even had the sleeves rolled up on his shirt. His forearms were very nice.

But she wasn't here to stare at his forearms. She was here to learn what she could about his ancestor and tour the part of the house that had once belonged to that witch.

She stretched out a hand when the silence between her and Miles grew ridiculous. "Lexie Alexander," she introduced herself. "I received your invitation." For a split second, as those words left her mouth, she thought, *Oh no, what if this isn't Miles, and I've not only embarrassed myself in the introduction, I've misjudged this entire situation?*

But then the man grasped her hand and shook gently and said, "Thanks for coming, Ms. Alexander. Miles Reid. Please call me Miles."

"Lexie," she offered in return. And ignored the little tingle as she slid her hand from his. Must be relief she hadn't started things off with a ridiculous mistake. And relief that the rumors about Miles appeared to be untrue.

"Thank you for coming," he said, then rocked back a little on his heels again. "I'm not sure where to start this." He blinked at her and then said, "Oh, sorry. Come in. Would you like something to drink?"

She smiled. "I'm good. Thank you. Why don't you start with why you sent me such a lovely, but vague, invitation."

The minute she stepped over the threshold of the house, something in Lexie tightened. A warning went up. And almost without meaning to, she started the spell for a shield, mentally reciting the words while she subtly moved her fingers in the gestures to fix the spell. She scanned the entrance as if some threat would leap out at her from behind the hallway table, or out of the huge mirror hanging over it, or from the closed door to the left, the minute Miles closed the front door. The punch of fear tightened her gut and shoulders.

But nothing happened. No deadly spells slammed into her. No monsters rushed from the shadows. Miles didn't suddenly transform into a different person.

She breathed through the shot of adrenaline and tried to let her muscles relax, tried to release the tension in her gut.

She did not stop the shield spell, though, finishing it with a little flick of her fingers, so that it was a little halo of blue light in her mind's eyes, shimmering and standing between her and the rest of the house.

Whether Miles sensed her immediate tension or whether he was just used to having to explain the house, he said, "This place can be a little…intense the first time you come in." He muttered, "Actually, that never gets easier." Then he shook his head. "But the…intensity wears off. A little." Clearing his throat, he gestured to the more Victorian side of the house. "Why don't we talk first? Then I'll show you the original section."

All her fear and caution got pushed aside at that offer. "Thank you. I'm really looking forward to seeing…her home." Witches didn't speak her name, those few who knew of her, but did his family say her name aloud? He'd included it in the invitation.

She followed him through a narrow open doorway just beyond the hallway table, a doorway she'd somehow managed to miss in her first frantic search after stepping inside.

The foyer was a relatively ordinary space, given the outside of the house. The solid wooden table, a large, unframed oval mirror over it, hardwood floors covered by a maroon-colored rug. The closed door to the left was a basic, white painted wooden door. Nothing elaborate. No ornate doorknob. No way into the house at the far end of the entryway, opposite the door, just a solid wall. No stairs. There weren't any pictures on the pale cream-colored walls. And no coat rack or random shoes at the door. Some mail scattered on the table, but nothing else. Bare, but still closer inside to a normal home than she'd anticipated. Like something she might walk into anywhere.

Until she stepped through the very narrow doorway on the right.

The hallway beyond was taller than the foyer, and narrower than was comfortable to walk through. She wasn't a tiny person, but she wasn't a huge person either, and she still felt like she had to suck in her shoulders and turn a little sideways to walk down the hall. Bit like walking down the narrow aisle on an airplane.

Here the walls had dark wooden wainscotting and a green velvet wallpaper above the wainscotting, giving the corridor a dark and oppressive feel. And there were only a few sconce lights along the wall to add any light at all.

Again, no paintings or art. No decorative additions like tables—which wouldn't have fit—and no doorways leading off the hall, which for some reason made it feel even more claustrophobic. No windows, even though she thought they were at the front of the house. No way out of the corridor except to turn around and go back, or keep marching head. They kept marching ahead.

But she did not drop her shield.

Ahead of her, Miles had his shoulders pulled up close to his ears and his head hunched a little forward, as if he felt the weird discomfort of the hallway, too. And maybe he did. He'd said the…intensity of the house never fully went away.

She had so many questions about this place now, she didn't even know where to begin.

The far end of the corridor let them out through another very narrow opening into a large sitting room that reminded Lexie of a big old Bed and Breakfast trying to be historically accurate. Large fireplace against one wall, delicate Victorian furniture with faded velvet covering. More dark wainscotting, though the wallpaper above was a lighter cream color here, which immediately brightened the room. The windows that looked out onto the driveway and the front porch were framed by long, green velvet curtains. The hardwood floor polished and covered with two Turkish rugs.

And for the first time, the smell of the house really sunk in for her. A strange smell that sort of crept up under her and took a while for her to identify. Or at least notice. She didn't actually know *what* she was smelling. A kind of musty scent, with some furniture polish mixed in maybe, but with a hint of a spice like sage, and underneath that maybe… Sulfur?

Her nose twitched. Ordinarily, her sense of smell was pretty bad. She barely noticed how things smelled, even bad things. So she was a little surprised she noticed something so subtle. But it still managed to slide up under her normally indifferent nose and punch her with foreboding.

This house was freaky.

"Is it always so…?" She started, then pressed her lips together. He hadn't even offered her a seat yet. Jumping into just how weird the house was and asking *why* it was so weird probably should wait on some of the formalities.

And there was also the little matter of *why* he'd invited her here to see the house. Miles didn't look like the spooky, mysterious owner she'd been expecting. But that didn't mean his motive here was harmless. And she needed to remember that.

Miles faced her, standing on the far side of a stiff-looking couch. "It's always like this, yes. Spooky and disorienting and the proportions change in every room. This is one of the few rooms that feels normal enough it doesn't keep you on edge the whole time."

"You live here full time?" What she really wanted to ask was *how*? How did he live here?

He sighed and nodded. "It's…part of the inheritance. I inherited the house from a cousin. Living here is…required."

"But you don't want to live here?"

"Would you?" he said, then shook his head. "Sorry. You don't even know…" He let out a long breath. "I'm getting ahead of myself. Can I offer you something to drink? Tea, coffee?"

She thought she heard him mutter, "Something harder."

That was the second time he'd offered her a drink in less than five minutes. Was that suspicious, or was he just nervous? "I don't want to put you to any trouble," she said.

Mostly because she wasn't sure she should eat or drink anything in this house. Part of her brain reminded her that was just in Faery. Another pointed out that the underlying smell in the place didn't make the thought of drink very appetizing anyway.

He gestured to one of the couches in the room. "I suppose I should explain myself and that invitation."

"Only if you want to." She tried to make herself comfortable on the stiff couch, but it wasn't easy. "You've lured me here with promises of exploring…her home. That was very good bait. Unless you have some sinister plot I should know about, explanations aren't necessary."

Her comment made him smile. He had a nice smile. Even if it didn't last long.

"I know the invitation was a little dramatic," he said. "I'm still not entirely sure why I did that except I was afraid you'd ignore an email. And I really need your help."

Her eyebrows popped up. "Help?"

"So, you've… You've felt how weird this house is? Just walking through it is off-putting. This is one of the few rooms in the house that I find bearable and even here…" He sighed. "That smell."

"I was wondering about that! What is it?"

"Got me. Permeates parts of the house. Other parts, nothing. Just an ordinary sort of house smell. There are places were its stronger and a lot lot worse. The sulfur undertone overpowers the sage and is gag-inducing."

Lexie considered him, and his relatively ordinary manner and appearance, his resigned tone. And finally had to ask, "Why do you live here if you find it uncomfortable?"

"Like I said, it's a requirement of the inheritance."

"Can't you just give up the house? Sell it to a historical preservation society?"

"No."

She waited for more of an explanation. When he didn't elaborate, she asked. "Was that part of the requirements of inheritance, too? Not turning the place into a museum."

"Not quite. I can't turn it into a museum and leave. It won't let me."

Well. That… She let out a slow breath. That didn't sound good. Either Mr. Miles Reid was not entirely in his right mind.

Or this house was cursed.

Her next breath turned to a sigh. Of course the house was cursed. Of course it was. This place had originally belonged to a witch who summoned demons in the name of revenge and then had to be killed by her own coven when the demon plague got out of hand. Of *course* her home was cursed. And Lexie should have expected that from the beginning.

Other things started to click in about the house then, so she asked, "The strange combination of architecture, the way this place is built so haphazardly? That's an attempt to contain…something? Isn't it?"

"You didn't comment on the fact that I said the *house* won't let me do what I want with it."

"It's a cursed house." She shrugged. "My first in person. But not unheard of."

He held himself so still for such a long moment, Lexie was a little afraid he was going to order her to leave. And then, like a pin prick in a balloon, he just deflated, relaxed, released such a huge sigh of air, she could practically see the tension ebbing away on that breath.

"Thank you," he murmured and half closed his eyes.

"For what?"

"For believing in something I can't explain and making that part so easy I'm a little dizzy." He opened his eyes fully and met hers. And she noted he had quite nice eyes. "I was afraid you'd think I was crazy and leave. But I need someone familiar with…her and her history. I need to figure out how to break this curse. I can't waste away here like my predecessors. I just can't. I need to find a way out of this house that isn't death and passing the place on to the next unlucky relative."

"Okay." She nodded, her gaze turned inward. "Okay, so let's start at the beginning."

"The witch."

"The witch. You don't say her name?"

"No one has in our family since her death. Why?"

"We witches don't say it either." She pressed her lips together and shrugged a little. "It's a bit like actors not saying MacBeth and calling it the Scottish play. Mostly superstition. I think. But given who she was and what she was capable of, the possibility that she set down some sort of curse that would fall on any witch who uttered her name isn't entirely implausible." She paused a moment, then said, "I'm assuming you realize I'm a witch?"

She'd leapt right in with complete honesty and a lot of

assumptions and was only just now realizing that might have been a misstep.

He settled her worries when he said, "That's why I ask you here, specifically. Not just because you were a historian of witchy things, but because you were also a witch. And it's taken me a while to track down someone like you. So, yeah, we don't have to dance around the subject. Magic and curses are real. I inherited a cursed house I have to live in until I die and pass it on, and it won't let me do otherwise. But I have to find a way to do otherwise. So I need the help of an expert in things both witchy and related to…her."

"Do you not invoke her name for superstitious reasons, or is there a real familial reason not to? Or is it the house? Does the house stop you?"

He smiled, just a little. "I can't believe what a relief it is to just talk about this stuff without having to prevaricate, hint, or insinuate, all without actually talking about the issue out loud. Thank you."

For some reason, his gratitude made her feel a little soft inside. She chose to worry about why later. After they assessed the curse. "Glad I could make at least a part of this easier. There's no need to pull your punches. I get it." She looked around the living room, with its mostly normal, if out-of-time, feel and its low-level bad smell. "I don't blame you for being desperate to get out of here." She met his gaze. "You can… You can leave the house, right?"

"I can. To work. To get groceries and stuff. Getting delivery people to come here is almost impossible. They get too near the house, freak out, and leave. I have to collect my mail and packages and things from a lockbox at the bottom of the hill."

She'd missed that on her drive up the roughly paved road to reach the house. But it made sense. After getting a good feel of the place, she wasn't surprised it drove away mundane people. She was a little surprised it hadn't driven her away.

"You're frowning," Miles said. "What's wrong?"

"I didn't have the same issue as your delivery people," she murmured, looking around the sitting room again. She'd had instincts screaming that she shouldn't be here. But her curiosity had overridden those instincts pretty thoroughly, even standing on the porch when she'd been closest to bolting. But not once had anything forced her to leave. "Nothing drove me away."

And now that she thought about it, now that she understood, that fact struck her as even stranger. She was here, at Miles's behest, to help uncover and maybe break the curse on this house. Wouldn't a cursed house want to scare her off so much her own curiosity would never hold out against the urge to run?

"Either the house thinks we'll fail and it's amusing itself," she said. "Or this is a trap for me as well as you."

"Or maybe it wants to be released?" Miles tried, leaning forward in his seat. He'd settled on the smaller settee across from the couch and the delicate piece of furniture looked barely able to hold him.

His hopeful tone hurt to hear. "Maybe," she allowed.

But that sort of magnanimous behavior wasn't typical of cursed houses in her experience. Not that she had firsthand experience. She'd never been in a cursed house or tried to break a curse on one before. She'd only studied them in historical records. A lot of the ones she'd encountered in those records had since been razed. And the ones that hadn't...

Well, she hadn't felt the overwhelming desire to visit them. Not until the arrival of a strangely formal, gold-lettered invitation to visit the former home of a notorious witch she'd been fascinated with for most of her adult life.

She'd practically run here. She couldn't have turned down that invitation if she'd tried.

And that was so suspicious now, in hindsight, Lexie lost her breath.

Shit. The *house* had lured her here.

CHAPTER THREE

"Please don't run away," Miles said, when he saw the look on Lexie's face. Her lovely eyes widened with some sort of realization. He could see that revelation spread over her expression. And he recognized only too well that look. The look that said she was in over her head and she had to get out of here immediately.

But if she left, he didn't know who else he could turn to. The fact that he could talk about this place so openly and without having to hedge around the realities of magic and a curse were such a relief he'd seen spots. He couldn't lose that now. At least not yet. Not until she'd seen the old part of the house, the original part. Not until they'd at least *tried* to find a way to break the curse.

He realized his desperation might drive her off as fast as whatever epiphany she'd just had. But he couldn't seem to rein in his feelings. He *was* desperate. He needed help.

He didn't reach toward her, or lean any farther forward, instead holding very very still as she stared at him, afraid if he moved, she'd bolt.

After a long moment, she blinked slowly and said, "The

house…" She swallowed and her hands clenched and unclenched on her large purse. "The house lured me here. It wanted *me* here. But why? How?"

Miles closed his eyes briefly and let out a soft, pained groan. "I've been researching, trying to find someone like you. The—" he cut off the epithet he was about to issue, afraid the house would take offense, "—house probably learned who you were through me. I'm so sorry. I had no idea it could do that. I have no idea what *it* is. The house repels others. But I didn't realize it would attract anyone. Hell, *I* don't want to be here. I just can't seem to *not* be here since inheriting. I leave and I feel compelled to come back no matter what. But it never occurred to me that would happen to someone who wasn't a relative and owner of the house."

He wanted to do something to reassure her. But what? The fucking house had lured her here. The weird gold-etched invitation made more sense now. His impulse to use it to intrigue her had seemed such a strange thing to do when he'd done it. But also logical. Part of him thought, yeah, this makes sense. I'll do this.

But maybe that wasn't *him*. Maybe that was the house convincing him the invitation was logical.

Followed on that thought, he wondered if Lexie *could* run away now. She wasn't a relative, even distantly—the genealogy of his family had been kept scrupulously over the years. Mostly, so the poor slobs who had to inherit the house could be identified. Lexie and her family weren't part of those records anywhere. The house wasn't part of her past, the way it was part of his. She shouldn't be trapped here the way he was.

But the *house* had also wanted her here.

Why?

"Why, though?" he asked aloud, though he was more asking the house than Lexie. "Why does it want you here?"

She shook her head slowly. "Do you know why this date is significant?" she asked, her gaze turned inward.

"The date?" He hadn't picked this date for any specific reason. He'd wanted to get Lexie here as soon as possible, but… "When I wrote out the invitation, it was just the date that came to mind. I thought… It was soon but not so soon you'd find it impossible to get here, not so soon you'd feel rushed. But not so far off you'd have time to change your mind if you decided to come."

She nodded absently. "It's the day she was killed. Your ancestor, the witch, died on this exact day, more than three hundred years ago."

Miles had no idea what to say to that. He felt a little like he'd been kicked in the gut. He probably should have realized. He knew the date she'd died. That was written into the family lore. But he hadn't realized…

Lexie focused on him for a moment, then dug into her purse. She carried a very large purse. He hadn't paid much attention to it earlier, but now that he watched her paw through it, he realized it was the size of a small backpack. A soft maroon leather with a thick strap she had crossed over her chest. As she dug into the depths, things clanked. What the hell did she have in there?

Finally, she pulled out a black leather notebook that looked well used. There weren't any markings on the book, but it had a long leather strap wrapped around it to keep it closed. She unwound the strap and opened the book, looking through it.

"These are all my notes on…her," she said without looking up at him. "Everything I've been able to uncover. Which is not very much for a notorious witch. I learned about her from my grandmother, before I started my research, but only the bare facts. I've been researching her for years. Unfortunately, a lot of the records have been scrubbed or hidden. But I've still found enough to know a lot of the details about what happened all those centuries ago." She glanced up. "Do you know her history? What she did? What happened to her?"

"She was a witch," he said with a shrug. "There're some rumors about demons. And I know her coven killed her. Just not…why."

"She unleashed a plague of demons onto the world in an effort to avenge the witches being killed, and tortured, and locked up during the witch trials. She was trying to destroy the fanatics persecuting the witches. I haven't been able to uncover if she lost control of the demons, or just got carried away with the murdering, but her coven was left no choice but to kill her to stop the plague."

"Now, wait, are we talking demon plague like…boils and illness and that kind of thing?" Miles sat up a little as dread washed through him. "Or…or real demons."

"Far as I can tell, real demons. From one of the demon realms."

"One of the—" He gulped. He actually gulped. Cursed house wasn't bad enough. Nope. Had to be demons. From more than one realm. Real ones, not just metaphorical ones. He'd always assumed the demons in the family curse were metaphorical.

He missed metaphor.

Releasing a long breath, he said, "Did a demon get trapped…in the house?" He was proud his voice didn't shake.

"Good question. I assumed all the demons were banished back to their realm. They would have had to have been or, well, they'd still be here. But maybe one got into her original house? Maybe one hid here all these years?"

"Oh good. A demon roommate. That's what I needed."

Her slight, wobbly smile at his sarcasm eased some of his growing anxiety. She had a really nice smile. And if the circumstances hadn't been so monumentally horrible, he'd have spent a little more time noticing that smile.

"I have no idea who banished the demons. I assume demon hunters since…well, that's their job. But any record of their participation in what happened has been cleaned or hidden or… I don't know. They might have just willed away any eyewitness's memory of the event."

"Willed away?" Demon hunters?

Okay, he'd been really relieved he could talk to someone about magic, and cursed houses, but Lexie was bringing up things that… He sighed. How did he go his whole life without knowing these things existed?

Lexie waved his question away. "Just a demon hunter thing. But now I think about it, if this place had an actual demon in it, the hunters probably would have found it by now. Right? It's not like the house has been moving around." She glanced at the ornate living room. "Why all the strange and chaotic construction, though?" She met his gaze. "What were your ancestors really trying to do here?"

That was at least something he could explain. "The earliest relative who inherited the house was also a witch, and he claimed in his diary that building around the original structure helped confuse and contain whatever curse was there. It was a way to trap it so it couldn't escape. Whatever *it* was. And he instructed the next person who inherited the house to keep building. What they built didn't matter, just that they built around the original structure. To hide it from the world and also confuse whatever it was that haunted the place."

He'd always assumed ghosts of some kind. But demons… Jesus, had they trapped a demon in the original cabin? Were his ancestors nuts?

"There's a house like that outside San Jose," Lexie said. "I haven't been, but the original owner just kept building and building. Doors and stairs that led nowhere. No real architectural plan."

"I've heard of the place." That particular mystery house was a big tourist attraction. When he inherited his own strange mystery house, it had been hard not to make the comparisons. Except he'd never risk turning this place into a tourist site. Him being here was bad enough. "As I understand it, the owner of that house built to keep spirits away. My ancestor insisted we build to keep…whatever this is in."

Lexie straightened a little. "Do you still add on to the house, build more around the original?"

"I haven't yet, but the last owner was still adding things. We don't own enough of the land around the place now to build out much. So the last cousin built small things like additional closets in weird places, like smack in the middle of rooms." He sighed. "I'll probably have to start that soon if I can't find a way to…end whatever is happening."

"If we can figure out how to stop the curse, what will you do?" Lexie asked quietly.

And something in her tone was so kind and understanding it made Miles's chest ache a little. He ignored the sensation. "I'll probably bulldoze the house and salt the ground and then move back to New York where I was living before inheriting." He glanced around. "There's nothing here I'd miss."

"Bulldoze it? Oh, that seems…" She bit her lip. "Sorry, but the historian in me balks at that idea. There's a lot of history here. Seems like it should be preserved."

"You're sitting in a room that smells low-level like sulfur and it's the least upsetting room in the whole house. Why would you *want* to preserve something so disturbing?" He was attached to the history of this place through family blood and he still didn't want it saved.

"It might feel less…oppressive once the curse is lifted," she said with a hopeful lilt to her voice that belied her wince.

Since he needed her help and didn't want to argue, he said, "I can't make any decisions until I figure out how to actually leave the house without feeling compelled to come back, so it's a moot point for now."

She nodded, but she nibbled her bottom lip as she glanced around the ornate sitting room. Then she looked down at the notebook in her lap. "So we can probably assume there isn't a demon trapped here—a real one—since the demon hunters haven't shown up." A crease formed on her brow. "Though as I understand it, they only show up when the demon is about to escape, so… So maybe if it's trapped, they let it be?"

Demon hunters again. He was having trouble getting over the fact that there was a job out there with the title "demon hunter," and it was a real job that people did because real demons from multiple realms not only existed but might try to get into this realm to kill people. That he might have a demon stuck in this house, that could get out if they tried to break whatever curse kept Miles there, was…

He wasn't sure how he felt about that.

"If it's a demon, and it's trapped by all the construction, and I try to break my connection to the house…" He met her gaze. "Am I going to release a demon plague like she did?"

Lexie shrugged, but the crease between her eyebrows

didn't go away. "Maybe. I don't really know." She lifted her notebook. "I don't have any information on that in here. Not specifically. I do know she issued a curse before dying because of course she did."

Her twist of irony forced a small smile from him, but he was too worried for the amusement to last longer than a split second.

"But I don't have exact records of *what* the curse was. No one recorded that." She frowned. "Which is kind of weird. Witches love to record the exact words and results of a curse. Depending on the witch, that record serves as warning not to issue curses or a template for future curses."

"Curses a big thing with you witches?" Miles asked. Then winced at his phrasing. "Sorry. I didn't mean *you* you. Just…"

She waved away his slip. "You're upset. No offense taken. Curses are a big thing with witches, but not necessarily casting them. They're within our…our magical range if you will. Wizards can't do them nearly so well and their curses are usually tied in with objects. They have to create something physical to contain the curse and carry it out."

Miles blinked at her a few times. Wizards, huh? Sure. Of course.

Cursed houses and witch ancestors obviously weren't enough to put him in the know. His research had been… lacking. Which he was actually more upset about than the fact that there were wizards in the world. He was a journalist and prided himself on accurate research. He'd failed to dig deep enough in his own case, only going so far as he needed to find Lexie. He probably should have probed this magical world a little more.

Desperation made him sloppy. He'd have to remember that.

"But for witches," Lexie continued, not noticing his stunned silence, "curses are really natural to us. Part of the package of our magic, if you will. No need to attach them to an object. And they don't even have to be person specific." She gestured to the house. "Sometimes they're tied to a lineage. But the fact that this curse is tied to *her* lineage is… strange. She wouldn't have cursed her own family." The crease was back between her brows. "Huh. Yeah, there's no reason she would have cursed her family. She'd have cursed the families of the witch burning fanatics, and maybe the families of her coven since they stopped her. But…why are her own relatives suffering?"

"Another witch cursed us?" Miles offered. "Her original home just carried bad…vibes or whatever and it's that we're containing in this monstrosity?"

"That last is possible. And whatever bad was there has leached into the rest of the house. Turning it into a…a thing with a mind of its own?" She winced and glanced around. "I really don't know for sure. And probably won't until I see the original part of the house. The curse she issued at death, that no one saw fit to record, probably wasn't a curse on her own family. Likely more a general, all-who-stop-me-will-suffer sort of thing." She frowned. "But maybe one of the coven members cursed her old home. Or maybe, like you said, there's just bad magic mixed into its foundations and that's what's hidden here."

"What do we do if it's bad magic?" He frowned. "Or a demon? What if it's one of those actual demons?"

"Maybe you should show me the original house now. There might be clues there."

He didn't miss the way she avoided answering his questions.

CHAPTER FOUR

exie followed Miles, still carrying her notebook on all things to do with the original owner of this house, and worried at the inside of her cheek with her teeth, which was a nervous habit she really had to break. Still, if there was ever a time to worry, this was it.

She'd come expecting to see a historic residence and maybe study some artifacts. None of what had happened since she knocked on the door of this place had followed the path she'd thought she was walking. Miles was not what she'd been expecting—he was a pleasant surprise—and the reason for her being here was not what she'd anticipated—a less pleasant surprise—and this house was an awful lot more than just a historic residence—a bad surprise.

The corridor Miles led her down was another awkwardly shaped one. Nothing a real architect would purposefully put into a house people were supposed to live in. The ceiling was low, not so low that she or Miles had to duck, but low enough it was noticeable and felt like she *might* have to duck at any moment. The walls were farther apart here, less of that walking down the aisle of an airplane feel to them, but in combination with the low ceilings, the width still felt... wrong. The walls were painted a dark green color and the parquet floor was bare. No tables, carpet runners, paintings, or decorations of any kind. And the overhead lights were recessed and gave the corridor a weird glow, almost like an office building.

She'd never been so relieved to move from one hallway to another. The small room they passed through was empty but for a single wall mirror opposite a window. There didn't seem to be any other lights in the room, just the mirror catching light from the bare window, casting enough reflection around the place to keep it bright. At least on a sunny day like today.

And somehow the fact that it was bright and sunny outside, and not dark and stormy, felt at odds with what she was doing. At odds with the house itself. The house seemed to demand darkly atmospheric weather.

Or maybe she was just being dramatic.

The next hallway was shaped almost normally. Not too tall, not too wide, a more Goldilocks hallway with proportions humans would be accustomed to. Another strange scent permeated the air here, though. Strong enough she noticed it even with her bad sense of smell. The hints of sulfur under it seemed old but all the more fetid because of it. And there was something else like burning plant material in the smell, but not the sort of pleasant-to-burn plant material. Not like a campfire, or a nice smelling herb. This was like someone burning stink weed or creosote in large quantities and then mixing in some volcanic rotten egg smell just for the fun.

Not a good smell.

She flexed her nostrils in an attempt to close them to the stench.

"Sorry about…" Miles waved his hand. "I've tried to find the source so I can…fix the smell. But whatever it is seems to be part of the corridor."

"Something died in the walls, maybe?" Which was a horrifying thought given everything else. Except, "Doesn't really smell like a dead animal, though, does it? Something weirder."

"Definitely weirder," Miles said. "I checked the walls." He shrugged a little. "I suppose I have done some building here. I hadn't considered that, but I did enough punching holes in walls, looking for the source of the stench, and then had to fix them. So I guess that counts as construction, right?"

He smiled at her over his shoulder, a little crookedly. And she had to smile back. If only they'd met under different circumstances. He'd even lived in New York. They could have met at a bar, or concert, or play, or anything else. Kind of sad they only met because he'd inherited a cursed house.

When they got to the end of the smelly hallway, they moved into a section that looked like it belonged in the castle wing. The floor turned to stone slabs with a long carpet runner down the middle of the room, stone walls hung with tapestries, wrought iron sconces burning pretend fire in between the tapestries, and thick wooden beams lining the ceiling.

"The decor fits the section of the house," she said, looking around.

"Sometimes. But there's a room in this wing filled with arcade games and a mini-movie theater so not always."

"You have a movie theater and an arcade in here somewhere?" Why did that strike her as really odd and whimsical? Probably because those seemed like fun things and there had been nothing about this house that felt fun so far.

"Not actually as cool as you might think," Miles said with a sigh. "There's no electricity in that part of the house, so the games can't work and there's no way to show a movie without a wireless projector which would be a lot of work, and who wants to go through that much trouble for a single person viewing."

"Always just one person living here? No families or anything?"

"Just one cousin, with no other family, inherits. Thankfully. It's not a safe house for kids. Too many weird rooms and closets and things. And any partner would probably immediately leave the poor bastard who'd inherited this place."

She stared at his back as he led her into another hallway —this one stone and narrow, with arched ceilings and a bare wooden floor. Had Miles had a partner before moving in here? Had he lost the potential of a family when he inherited this place?

She didn't ask those questions, because they didn't know each other well enough for that. But she did wonder.

After another couple of uncomfortable, but blessedly short hallways, Miles finally stopped at a stone wall that seemed to lead nowhere. A dead end.

He turned to face her. "I haven't actually been in this part of the house in a while. I only went in once. I know what's in there. But I couldn't go back after the first look."

"Because something in there is bad?"

"Because every time I tried, the house turned me around and I'd end up somewhere else. It didn't let me back."

She glanced past him at the blank stone wall. "Is that what just happened? Are we lost or turned around or…"

"No. We're here." He pointed over his shoulder. "That's

got a secret door in it. I'll open it in a minute. I just…wanted to prepare you."

"What's on the other side."

"The witch's cottage. It's enclosed in stone and wood now. The windows are covered. There's no view of the outside. And there's more construction over the top of the house. But the original cottage is intact. And it looks pretty much as she left it."

A part of Lexie rejoiced at the thought, at being able to see exactly how and where the witch had lived. To see her furniture, her belongings, maybe find some of her books. The historian in her could hardly wait.

The more cautious part of her thought maybe going into that space would be a bad idea.

But since she couldn't explain *why* she was worried, she pushed the worry aside. She'd come all this way to see this place. She wasn't about to turn back now.

Especially now that she knew Miles was trapped with this house. They needed to find a way to release him from it. Without saddling some other poor cousin with the place.

"Are you ready?" Miles asked.

"One minute." She'd dropped her shield spell earlier, while they were in the sitting room talking, when she was certain nothing would jump out at her from the shadows. Now, just in case, she thought having that shield in place again might be a good idea. For both her and Miles.

The instinct to believe him, to trust that this wasn't some elaborate trap of some kind, fed her need to protect him. She'd spent her whole life trusting her instincts about people. They'd never once let her down.

She'd trust them now. Because her instincts were all she really had.

She tucked her notebook back into her bag so her hands

would be free, and then she murmured the spell, forming the few gestures with her fingers required to set the spell. When she flared her hand out, the shield flashed blue in her mind's eye, a half sphere of light in front of her.

To Miles, she said, "Okay, I'm ready. But once you've opened the door, move behind me. Just in case."

"Why?" He frowned at her, looking at her hand. She held it in front of her, palm facing the wall, holding the shield in place, because unlike her earlier one, this one was designed to protect her and Miles. But since he wouldn't be able to see the magic, the hand gesture probably looked strange.

"I've built a shield against a magical attack," she said, motioning a little with the hand holding the shield. "You'll be safer behind me and this until we're sure there's nothing… dangerous on the other side of that wall."

"I've been in there before. There's nothing…nothing obviously dangerous." Still, he glanced between her and the door. "But I'm not one for unnecessary risks."

She smiled a little, brows raised. "No jumping out of perfectly good airplanes?"

"No skydiving. No bungy jumping. No climbing Mount Everest." He smiled and shrugged. "I get enough of an adrenaline rush hunting down a story."

Lexie realized she'd liked to talk to him about that more. About his job. His hobbies. The things he liked and hated.

But they weren't on a date, getting to know each other, asking all those kinds of questions. They were standing just outside the house of a witch who'd summoned demons and whose relatives lived under some sort of curse tied to this house. She was here to help with that mess.

The fact that she liked the current owner of the house and wanted to get to know him better was… Well, not something she could worry about in that moment. But she might think about it later.

If they got out of this.

"Ready?" she asked him this time.

He pulled in a deep breath, nodded, then pressed a stone on the wall that looked like every other stone on the wall.

This stone, however, moved inward with a release of air. And then the stone wall swung open like a door.

Miles moved behind her. They both stared at the darkness beyond that rectangular gap in the wall.

"We need a light?" she asked. She could make a magical light to illuminate the space if they needed it. But she wasn't a powerful enough witch to hold that spell and her shield spell at the same time. She'd need to drop the shield if they needed a magical light.

And in this case, she thought they were better off with her shield and a more mundane illumination option like a flashlight.

"We won't need it," he said. "You'll see when we walk in."

Okay. That sounded creepy. And also fascinating.

Her curiosity overwhelmed her hesitance, again, and she finally moved forward, leading the way into the long dead witch's cottage.

CHAPTER FIVE

he first thing Lexie noticed was the fire in the fireplace. An actual fire burned in a stone fireplace at the opposite end of a large, open room. There was no wood under the fire. It burned on top of a metal grate, dancing in its red and orange and yellow light. Without any visible source of fuel. Smoke rose up a chimney that may or may not have actually led outside.

"The chimney?" she asked, her voice very quiet.

"Blocked off. Long time ago. Didn't do a thing to stop the fire."

Yet no smoke filled the room. And the whole place hadn't burned down. Which it probably should have. If that was a normal fire.

"How long?" she asked, her voice still barely a breath.

He didn't ask what she meant. "Since she was killed. Or so the lore goes. That fire has never gone out, even after the chimney was blocked and the wood that had originally fed it burned up."

"Not once? In more than three hundred years?"

"Not once. In more than three hundred years."

"That's…"

"Bad. Scary. Weird. Terrifying."

"All of the above," she said.

"Yup," Miles said.

Keeping the shield firmly in front of her and Miles, Lexie finally took in the rest of the room.

A single open space. Hardwood floors that were rough but remarkably dust free. No rugs or anything to soften the floors. A single wooden bed up against one wall, a straw stuffed mattress and a homespun blanket across it. A wooden trunk at the base of the bed. A table and shelves near the fireplace for preparing and cooking food. There were still bottles of herbs up on the shelves, and a few that look to be distillations of some kind. But given the three hundred year old fire, Lexie had no desire to explore what was inside those bottles after all this time.

Her nose twitched, as if anticipating very bad smells from the bottles, even though the cabin itself didn't have a very strong odor—at least not that she could pick up. No strong dust or dirt smells. No sulfur like in other parts of the house. Nothing came from the fire. A faint sort of mustiness, maybe? She was so bad with smells. It wasn't like being in a preserved museum room, though. There wasn't a smell of "old" here. Which was as strange as the fire.

A door opposite the bed and another at the back of the house probably led to either closets or another room. Though she thought the back door might also have once led out of the cottage. She could imagine an herb and vegetable garden just out that door, the image leaping into her mind as if she'd seen it before. A place once circled by trees, enough space behind to grow the things a witch would need to heal and help her community.

All the things that would later be used against her by religious fanatics.

The fire cast dancing yellow shadows around the room. With the windows blocked, knowing there was construction overhead, she felt like she was inside a cave, a room built inside a cavern, and the sense of claustrophobia was stronger than she would have anticipated. The whole place had a sort of oppressive feel, like the cabin resented being cut off from the world and would ensure anyone who came inside felt that oppressive weight.

"Where do we start?" she asked. A part of her was waiting for something to…happen. She wasn't sure what. Something to jump out at them from the shadows. A sense of foreboding crawled along her spine, making her edgy and ready to run.

"Maybe the trunk?" Miles pointed to the large wooden box at the base of the bed. "I never opened anything in here. Came in, saw the fire, left. Haven't been back."

"Can't blame you," she muttered under her breath. She was a witch. She was used to magic. And that fire still bothered her. "Okay. Trunk seems a good place to start. Maybe she left a journal or some writings of some kind."

"Do you believe in ghosts?" he asked quietly.

She looked over her shoulder at him. "Yes. But maybe not in the traditional sense? I see them as energy remains. The stronger the energy, the more likely there is to be…lingering parts left behind."

"I came across that thinking in my research. I'm not sure if I believe in ghosts or not. I've never seen one. But I believe in malevolent energy because I live in a house full of it."

"Do you think she's…here?" Lexie resisted the urge to glance into the shadows, looking for the specter of his witchy ancestor, but the fine hairs on her neck rose and a little shiver she couldn't contain moved through her.

She'd come here hoping to see this place, to explore *her* original home. She hadn't come here anticipating a confrontation with *her*.

"I don't know what's here." He nodded at the fire. "But whatever it is, it isn't…ordinary."

No. Not ordinary. Her gaze flicked to the fire, burning all these years without fuel, sending smoke up a chimney with no opening to the outside, and yet none of that smoke backing up into the cabin.

She kept her shield raised as they approached the bed. She wanted to keep the protective barrier between them and the trunk when they opened it, in case there were any dangerous traps inside.

"Has anyone ever opened anything in here? The trunk?" she asked, staring down at it. It was large, flat topped, wooden, held closed with two leather straps clipped into place by large brass clip locks. Like a steamer trunk. The leather didn't look dried out. The wood wasn't warped by time. The brass looked bright and clean.

The way time seemed to have stood still inside this place was disturbing as fuck.

"As far as I know," Miles said, "no one has. At least not that they've written down anywhere for the rest of us. But there haven't been a lot of warnings left to new owners from previous owners. I'm…not really sure why. If I can't break the curse and get out of here, I'm definitely leaving a lot of written warnings for the next poor person who has to take on the house."

"There could be traps," she said. "So stay behind me and the shield." Her shield was designed for magical issues, and wouldn't do them much good against an aerosol poison or something like that. But since she suspected anything in here would be magic based, she hoped the shield would prevent disaster.

Reaching through her shield to open the trunk was interesting. Her skin tingled against the energy in the shield, the feel of her own magic. And there was a sense of resistance in it, like it was trying to keep her from moving any part of herself out from behind its protections.

She flicked the two brass locks open. Waited for something bad to happen. When nothing did, she lifted the lid. It was heavy and awkward to pull up one-handed, but she didn't want any more of her body outside her shield than was necessary, and at any rate needed her other hand to continue holding the shield in place.

With a grunt, she got the lid all the way up, tossing it a little to get it fully raised. Then she drew her hand quickly back behind her shield. She wasn't looking at him, but she swore Miles stopped breathing behind her as they waited.

Finally, after a few moments, when it was clear nothing was going to spring at them from inside the trunk, they both leaned forward to look inside.

Lexie wasn't sure why but the piles of clothes and linens in the chest surprised her. Yet, where else would the witch have kept her linens? The fact that they were perfectly preserved and didn't appear to have aged shouldn't be surprising either in a room with a fire that had been burning for more than three hundred years.

"I'm going to lower the shield," she murmured, glancing around the room one more time. "I think we're okay."

Miles nodded, but didn't comment.

She dropped her shield spell, waited a beat to make sure all was safe, then dropped to her knees in front of the trunk and slowly started shifting aside the material.

As a historian, getting this kind of glimpse into a famous —or in this case infamous—person's ordinary life was pretty amazing. And this was the very thing that had drawn her here, this ability to see things actually owned by that long ago witch, to feel the things she'd felt and touched. She wasn't herself a touch psychic who might pick up visions from handling these things, but she didn't need that. She just like knowing she was in the presence of things that had a history.

Most of what was inside the trunk was ordinary women's clothing from the late seventeenth century. Some shifts and drawers and skirts, some shirts and a few bonnets. Nothing fancy but all of it was well made, nothing frayed or in need of repairs that hadn't already been done. There were some stockings at the bottom of the trunk, and a pair of leather shoes that looked durable if a little less comfortable than her own sneakers. And next to the shoes, beneath underclothing and a soft homespun blanket, rested a book.

Not the ominous black leather or skin-wrapped book one might expect from a notorious, demon-summoning witch. No, this one was wrapped in a green fabric that was rough against her fingertips, but not unpleasantly so. The spine was thick. There weren't any symbols or markings on the cover, nothing to indicate if it was a book or a journal or even a recipe book. Given the owner of this book was a witch who had bottles of things on her shelves, Lexie would have bet money it was some sort of recipe book, but the kind unique to a witch.

She'd have won her bet, too.

Carefully opening the pages, she scanned the elegant scrawl of handwritten notes.

"What is it?" Miles asked, leaning over her shoulder.

"Recipes," she murmured, her finger running across the page.

"For food?"

"Some actually, but mostly for…potions. Things a local midwife or witch might make. Concoctions to help headaches, stomach ache, poultices for wounds, methods for setting bones, things to help against infection." She glanced back at him. "She was a healer, it looks like. Originally anyway. But a woman doing that kind of work would have drawn the attention of…well, religious fanatics." She shook her head. "Always the women trying to do good, the ones the fanatics didn't understand or like."

"But she wasn't brought before the witch trials," Miles pointed out. "She wasn't accused of witchcraft by the powers that be."

"That we have a record of." But maybe he was right. She was notorious for unleashing demons on the witch-killers. Not for being accused of witchcraft herself. "At any rate, most of this is ordinary healer stuff. Notes and methods and potions and herbs and lists of options for dealing with ailments of all kinds."

"So, nothing that will help us end whatever curse is on the house." Miles groaned, the sound so full of frustration Lexie winced.

"We'll find something," she said, trying to reassure him.

As she flipped through more recipes and notes, a loose sheet of paper drifted from the book, falling back inside the half-empty trunk. Lexie frowned and picked it up, gently setting the book back into the trunk. She unfolded the page, and gasped.

A full diagram, with illustrations and annotations…

Of a demon realm.

CHAPTER SIX

*L*exie couldn't quite believe what she was seeing. Mainly because she'd never encountered a document that actually illustrated a demon realm before. And on the face of it, the document was so ordinary, too. No skins. No blood for ink. Just ordinary seventeenth century paper with ordinary seventeenth century ink, fully diagraming out a complete demon realm.

All of it. The types of demons there. Their skills and strengths—which were many. Their weaknesses—which were few. The drawings were grotesque reflections of horrifying entities, and the page was difficult for her to look at directly. Her eyes kept trying to avoid the paper even though it was right in front of her. To study it, she had to look at it from the corner of her eye. And even then, her brain didn't want to acknowledge what it was seeing, or read the writing on the page.

"Can you look directly at it?" she asked Miles. This belonged to one of his ancestors after all. Maybe it was more difficult to read if you weren't related.

"Only in short bursts. Then my mind starts screaming and I have to look away."

"Okay. Well, I think we found something significant."

"But can it help us break the curse of this house or is it just another weird artifact like the fire?"

She had no idea.

She focused on reading the writing at the edges of the page. But doing that from the corner of her eye proved difficult, given the writing was mostly in Latin and she couldn't look at it directly. She'd studied Latin in college when getting her history degree. It was a language she felt comfortable interpreting. And yet, she had a lot of difficulty reading the inscriptions along the edge of the paper. The words kept swirling and blurring.

"Damn it," she muttered. "Can you read Latin?"

"Not even a little bit. I know *carpe diem*, but that's about it."

"Did any of your ancestors, the ones who owned this house after her, especially the one who claimed there had to be constant building to contain whatever was in here... Did any of them speak Latin?"

"No idea for the last few people. The first witch, I assume he did because some of the writings he left were translated from Latin."

She glanced back at Miles. "Do you have the originals in Latin? Or only the translations?"

"Both. But there wasn't anything in them about how to break the curse on the house. Someone would have done it by now."

"I was mostly wondering if he could have read this document if he'd found it. If anyone could."

"Can you?"

"I read Latin, fluently. But I'm having trouble here—I

can't look directly at the page, and the words I can see from the corner of my eye keep…I don't know. Flowing away from me when I try to focus on them."

"The first witch to own this place after her, James Lacey, he would have gone through her stuff. He might have found this. If he did, and there was a way to break the curse with it, wouldn't he have done that?"

"Maybe," she said, but maybe not. If he couldn't read the document any better than she could, or if he didn't try because of…well, what it was and what *she* had done, then maybe he wouldn't have known if it was useful.

"Should you be trying to read it?" Miles asked. "I mean, maybe it summons demons instead of banishes them."

She let out a long breath. He wasn't wrong to worry about that. "If I don't read it, though, or if I can't, we won't know if there's a clue here. She had to have left something. Why would she condemn her own relatives to this place?"

"She summoned a demon plague on innocent people. I'm not sure she would have cared about her ancestors."

"Not innocent people," Lexie said, hearing a slight bite in her voice. "The fanatics killing witches were not innocent people. Some of the ones they killed weren't even really witches. And those people died in horrible ways."

Miles was quiet a moment. Then, "I'm sorry. I didn't mean to imply… Well, I'm sorry. She had a right to her anger. I realize that. But obviously, her methods of revenge were bad, or her coven wouldn't have killed her."

Lexie had to agree. But the motivation behind the act… well, she understood that only too well. "Pull my notebook out of my bag, the one with my notes on her, please."

He gently opened her purse and reached in. Given the depths of her bag and the array of things she carried, she wasn't surprised he rooted around so delicately. But it did amuse her.

When he had the notebook, she said, "I need to check something. Could you flip it open until you find a picture of a tree?"

"Drawing or photo?" he asked as he started flipping pages.

"Drawing."

She noticed him pausing frequently to read, and really couldn't blame him. The information was fascinating. Or at least it was to her, as a history keeper. As an ancestor, she had to assume the details were fascinating to him too, but maybe for a different reason.

"Found it yet?" she asked even as she continued trying to read the document and having very little luck.

"This it?" He turned the notebook so she could see the image.

"That's the one."

It was a drawing of a large, sturdy oak with multiple branches and a trunk split into a V-shape. In the drawing, the leaves of the oak were mostly gone, except for a few stragglers at the edges, leaving the long branches bare. The whole thing was very ominous looking. Especially because the artist had drawn in a noose hanging from one branch, like a warning.

She realized, with a shock, that the date on the drawing, the date that had been on the original that she'd copied into her notebook…

That was today's date.

The date the witch had been killed.

She'd never realized, never noticed… "There's an inscription at the bottom of the image," she said. "Could you read it out loud for me, please."

He was silent for a long time. Then, "'Whomsoever reads from this tree, ye shall know the way. And whomsoever reads from the product of this tree, so too shall ye know the way.'" Miles fell silent again for a few moments before finally asking, "What does that all mean?"

"I think it means this paper—" she lifted the document illustrating the demon realm, "—is made from oak wood, and that I need to read it." She kept most of her focus on the swirling words on the document as she spoke. "That tree drawing and the inscription? She was buried in an unmarked grave by her coven, so we don't know where her body is. But they left this memorial, a sort of warning I think, at the site of the…incident. There was an oak tree there, like the one in the drawing. And they put up a stone marker with this exact drawing and inscription on it. Along with the date."

"You think the demon realm document is something she made, or something her coven made?"

"I think it's something she made. I think it's a link to the way she was able to unleash demons. I'm not sure exactly how she did it—no one has ever recorded how she managed it in any of the writings, and if there's someone out there I can ask, they're not making themselves known." Though she suspected the demon hunters had more information. They definitely weren't talking about it. At least not to her. "But I think it links to this oak tree in some way. I think the oak tree links to this document. And I think the answer to the…curse, the haunting, the strangeness of this house of hers is found in this document."

"I think we should burn the document," Miles said suddenly.

And they both glanced at the three hundred year old fire.

But everything in Lexie balked at the idea. Burning a valuable historical document? Something likely made specifically for this purpose, hand drawn, something that had been touched by a witch she'd been researching for years? A large part of her screamed, *No*!

Yet…

Another, smaller part of her whispered, *yes*.

She shook her head. "That might make things worse. We don't know yet. I need to be able to read the document."

"I still can't look at it very long. Can you?"

Frustrated, she said, "No. That's the problem."

She held the page at a different angle, letting it catch the light from the fire more directly. That firelight was their only source of illumination, and it cast shadows across the paper that made the demons appear to dance and move. The text on the page seemed to move, too. And nothing stayed still or in focus long enough for her to catch more than a word or two.

"Maybe we're not supposed to read it? Or maybe not meant to?" she murmured. "Maybe only a specific person or witch could do it?"

"If that's the case, I'm stuck in this house until I die, and I'm not accepting that, so we have to figure this out."

She heard his desperation and growing anger. She couldn't blame him. For all her interest, her fascination with this particular witch, she most certainly wouldn't want to be trapped in this strange and disorienting house for the rest of her life.

Lexie looked at him. His jaw was tight and he was still taking quick, passing glances at the document. She waited for him to meet her gaze. Then said, "We'll figure it out. We will." She scanned the room. "Maybe I need a different source of light."

"There's not exactly electricity back here."

"Not the kind of light I was thinking of."

She gently set the document down in the trunk, on top of

some of the clothes and linens still inside, so she could have her hands free. Then she quietly murmured the words for the light spell, her fingers twining in a pattern to set the spell. With a last, whispered word, she flicked her fingers wide and up. Over her head, a soft blue ball of light formed, the color slowly swirling until it was casting a gentle blue-white glow across the room.

The shadows surrounding them pushed back into the corners, behind the sparse furniture, up onto the shelves. And with that additional light, the cabin itself felt infinitely less oppressive. Even the flickering glow from the fire seemed less ominous, less overpowering.

"Better," she said as she picked up the document again.

"Wow. Yeah, that's a lot better. Better than the flashlight I brought back here that first time. Should I ask how you did that?"

"Same way I built the shield. I thought you understood magic."

"I know it exists and I know about witches with magic. I don't understand everything that can be done with magic."

"Do you want to?" she asked, genuinely curious.

Most mundane humans who had to deal with magic fell into two categories. They wanted it for themselves. Or they wanted to run away from it, as far as they could get. She wondered which kind Miles was. Though, up to now, his primary associations with magic involved an ancestor killed by her own coven for misusing her magic, and a magic house that kept the owners of it virtual prisoners for their entire lives. If he wanted magic for himself, she'd be surprised.

"Honestly?" he said. "I'm fascinated enough to want to know more, but in an abstract way. I'd rather not be in the middle of…" He gestured at his surroundings.

"Understandable." She pointed to the light overhead with one hand. "But sometimes magic is useful."

He nodded, also looking up at her little ball of illumination. "Definitely useful in making this place feel less…" He shrugged. "Less."

She looked back at the document, still from the corner of her eye, but now under the better light. The images on the page stopped dancing. She still couldn't look directly at it, but things weren't swirling around as much.

So, the trick was not to look at it in firelight. "Wonder if we could take it out of here?" she said, mostly to herself. "If I could look at it in daylight, would that help?"

"Is your own light helping?"

"A lot. That's what made me wonder."

"The witch who inherited this place first, James Lacey… He said we shouldn't remove anything from the cottage. To do so would risk freeing more demons." Miles glanced at the document. "I suppose he meant that literally. He was worried we'd loose demons the way she did."

Was that a risk Lexie was willing to take? Probably not. She had no way to return demons to their realm if she accidentally set any free. And she really didn't want to accidentally set any free.

Her gut tightened. What if reading the document did just that? What if they were, quite literally, playing with fire?

She let out a slow breath. This was their only clue. She had to try. And hope.

Concentrating, she focused on the document again, letting her peripheral vision take in the words scrawled around the edges of the page. The elegantly looped handwriting matched what was inside the recipe book. This was made by the same hand who'd written the book. At least… The outer inscription was hers.

Some of the words started to come into focus as she stared ahead while reading from the corner of her eye. She hesitated to read the words aloud, though. Just in case.

"They're starting to coalesce," she said to Miles.

"Read them."

"Not out loud. Might be a spell. I might…trigger something. But it says the demons come from the tree and were banished back to the tree."

"The oak tree?"

"Maybe. Doesn't make sense." She frowned and turned the document as she followed the writing. "I'm getting the impression this page, made of that oak wood…contains something."

"As in there's something in the document?"

"No, the document…prevents it from being released. But…" She frowned. Most of the words were in Latin but some were in old English and the mix was difficult to decipher. "But release is the only answer?" She shook her head. "I think I'm translating that wrong. Give me a minute."

The difficult thing about Latin was that there were different translations for words depending on context, and that context here was complicated by old English words thrown into the mix. She had no confidence in her interpretation. But…

Even if she tried other variations, it came down to… "This seems to be saying, the demon must be released to be banished? I… I'm not sure that makes sense."

"Releasing a demon seems like a bad idea," Miles said. He tried glancing directly at the paper then made a frustrated growl and looked away.

"It might be the only option if you want whatever's turned this house into a prison to end. From what I can tell, there's…something here. Something that's part of the document but also the bones of the house. And it's something that needs to be released or it will just linger here."

She stopped trying to read the document and looked at Miles directly. "I can see why James Lacey thought the only way to deal with this was contain it, build around it, confuse it and ensure it stayed trapped and buried. But burying it gave it time to…leach through to the rest of the house. It turned the rest of the house into a sort of… A shrine to *her* anger. It was her anger that set her on the path to releasing the demon plague. And it's her anger that's trapped here in the bones of this cabin. Her anger that's leached through to the rest of the house. That's what needs to be freed, to be released, so the house can rest."

"How? How do we do that without unleashing demons on the world?"

She let out a sigh. "The how is the problem. That's why James Lacey went a different route. I can't blame him. I don't want to do this either."

"Do what?"

"Call up the demon of her anger. Bring it physically into this world. Here. In the cabin."

"And let it kill us? I'm not sure how that helps."

"Once it's here, we burn the document. She always meant for her anger to be cleansed and the document burned. At least that's what I'm getting from the writing. The process to *clean* this place of what's making it so bad is to release her anger from it, and then burn the document."

They both glanced at the fire.

"We can't burn the document first?"

"If we do that, we destroy any hope of releasing her anger and ending what's made this house a prison for you. You'll be trapped."

"You're sure?"

She had to be honest. "No. I can't be absolutely certain because we're talking about a three hundred year old document written in two different archaic languages. Because even the first witch to inherit this place chose not to do this and to try something else. But the something else isn't working. The building didn't bury the…the demons here. It only let them fester. Grow. Contained them to this one place, yes, but didn't banish them." She met his gaze again. "We have to banish the anger if you want to be free."

"Her anger was…huge. And righteous even if her actions weren't."

"Yes."

"What if it overwhelms us before we destroy the document?"

"That would be bad," she said.

"Helpful."

"I'm not going to sugarcoat this. If this was easy, your ancestor would have done it three hundred years ago, and we wouldn't be here right now."

He held her gaze for a silent moment. Something she couldn't read moved through his expression. Then he blinked and shook his head, muttering something under his breath she couldn't hear.

Louder, he said, "It's either this or I stay trapped and keep building to keep whatever is here from leaking out beyond the house. Those are my options?"

"Yes." And his choice. She couldn't make the choice for him. She wasn't sure she wanted to do this herself. She was scared of what they'd unleash. But if he chose to try, she'd help.

Because he was right. That long ago witch, her anger had been righteous. And justified. And now it needed to rest. Anger left to fester too long was a kind of rot that was baked into the walls here now. That rot had to be cleaned out. Finally. For everyone's sake.

"Okay." Miles glanced between the document and the fire. "Okay. I can't stay here and do nothing. I don't want to face an end like the cousin I inherited the house from. We have to at least try."

She nodded. "Okay then. First…we need a circle."

CHAPTER SEVEN

Lexie wasn't sure how else to do this in a semi-safe way. There was no telling what would happen when they let the ephemeral energy of the anger trapped in this house coalesce into a physical form. But she doubted it would be good. And they would need to survive that summoning long enough to burn the document and release the energy.

To do that, they needed to do the work from inside a proper protective circle.

Under the blue-white glow of her magical light, with the more than three hundred year old fire flickering behind her, she silently drew a circle around her and Miles in the center of the cabin where they'd cleared space. First, she drew the outline with chalk from her bag. Then she layered on a sprinkle of salt—also from her bag—on top of the chalk. Then she quietly murmured the finishing spell and closed her eyes to visualize following the line of chalk and salt with her magic. When the ends of the circle came together, a flare of blue light in her mind's eye assured her it was set.

"Okay," she said, opening her eyes and readjusting the

strap of her bag across her chest where she'd settled it so she'd have her hands free. "Don't cross the chalk line. No matter what. If you break the line, you'll break the spell and we won't have the protection of the circle anymore."

"The fire is outside the chalk circle," Miles pointed out.

She'd drawn the circle as close to the fire as she dared, but the physical parts of the circle couldn't go around the back of the fireplace. There were witches who could draw a protective circle without needing the physical anchors in this realm—the chalk and salt. But she wasn't one of them. At least not for this level of circle. She needed the physical anchors to really set the spell solidly. And she didn't dare do a half-assed job in this case.

Also, *including* a more than three hundred year old fire *inside* the circle felt…counterproductive to protection.

"We'll have to break the circle to burn the document," she said. "But we'll survive long enough to do that if we do the other working from inside the circle."

Mile swallowed loud enough she heard it.

Her own nerves danced and fear crawl through her gut. She was terrified her circle wouldn't hold, that whatever they were about to release would overwhelm them. That she'd get Miles and herself killed because she'd miscalculated… something. But her instincts said this was the only way out for him.

And maybe it was the only way out for that demon-summoning witch, too. Her anger had lived on in this house for so many years. Centuries. It was time to put that to rest.

Lexie had been drawn to this house, to Miles's invitation. She'd felt the need to be here. Either the house wanted her to do this, or it had brought her here for a more nefarious reason. She was going with her instincts, and with release.

And hoping her instincts didn't fail her.

She held up the document, able to look at it a little easier now that they were inside the circle, which surprised her. She still couldn't look at it directly for long, but she could at least see the words when she looked at it directly. If she moved her head a little, looking at the writing from off center but not as far as from the corner of her eye, she could read it. Silently, she went through all the text again, hunting for a catch, a misinterpretation. A word that's differing definitions could change the entire meaning of what was written.

Nothing so far off that her original interpretation had to change.

She nodded. "Okay, there's a…a spell buried in here," she said. She felt Miles come up next to her, warm and comforting. She blinked a little at realizing having him close was comforting. He was a stranger. That seemed weird. "I'm going to recite the spell." She reread it in her head. "I… Most of my spells also require corresponding hand gestures. This one doesn't seem to. Just a straight read and add some magic and it should work."

"How do you add some magic?"

"That part comes from my…my core if you will. It's hard to explain. It's part of me and I just need to channel some of it into working this spell."

"Could I have done the spell—if I recognized it, and had been able to figure it out—could I have done this without actual magic?"

She shook her head. "I don't think so. This one needs a witch with magic. Even a well-studied non-magical witch wouldn't have what was needed to make this work."

"Then I'm glad I found you," he said quietly. "Even if I'm sorry I put you into this situation."

She smiled, her gaze darting to his briefly. "If this works, you can buy me a drink."

"Dinner, many drinks, and a car," he said. With feeling.

She chuckled. Then let out a slow breath and focused again on the writing. "Here we go."

Under her breath, quiet at first, she began reciting the spell aloud. Slowly, careful of her pronunciation the first time through, making sure she could say it correctly all three times.

It wasn't a long spell. A four line couplet of poetic Latin. No old English here. Just the Latin. And the rhyme. And the trickle of power she let run into the first reading.

More power into the second, her voice louder. She felt the rise of her magic, the way it moved through her chest, adding depth and resonance to the words as she repeated them.

Third time, louder, faster, more power. Stronger. Insistent. All her intentions poured into completing the spell.

On the last word, her voice echoed around the small cabin, bouncing around the low wooden rafters, swirling around inside the circle.

She held her breath. Miles moved closer to her side, their arms touching now as they watched. Waited.

"There!" Miles pointed to an area opposite the fire, outside their circle.

A coalescing of...fog? She wasn't sure. Not real fog obviously. Not smoke. A faint, acrid scent filled the cabin. Not sulfur, but bitter and harsh. Chemically. Her nose twitched, and she very much missed her usual inability to smell much.

The bitter flavor crept through the room as the white fog formed into a vaguely human shape. Impossible to tell anything about the shape beyond a vague form of head, shoulders, arms. No legs. Just smoke.

The form folded and reformed, until the top part of the shape grew more solid. Now Lexie could see something like long hair around the shoulders. And a red glow burned in the area where the eyes were.

She had to remind herself this wasn't that long-ago witch. She'd died more than three hundred years ago. This was the manifestation of her anger. Her personal demons. Not even a real demon.

At least, Lexie hoped this wasn't a real demon. She was not equipped to fight off a real demon.

A face, blurred and melting, formed in the head. Glowing red eyes. A mouth that, when opened, revealed more glowing red inside. In the area where a nose would have been, steam poured out in intermittent puffs.

Miles gripped Lexie's arm—the one not holding the document—and she leaned closer to him.

The mouth in the specter opened wide, too wide for a real human. Lexie winced, expecting some sound, a scream or screech. But the wail was silent. Horrifyingly silent.

The being, whatever it was, grew as it howled in silence, growing thicker and larger, and the white fog started to glow everywhere red. And as it solidified, and grew, the vaguely human shape transformed again. Horns rose up from its head. Bat-like wings spread out from its back, forming a kind of halo around the form.

"That's looking like a real demon," Miles murmured.

"Little bit," she agreed.

"Is it?"

She didn't think it was supposed to be, but... "Don't know. Could be."

"Will this work?"

"We're about to find out."

The creature, manifestation, whatever it was, turned its burning gaze on them, and its wings spread out behind it and the mouth hinged open farther and still the scream was silent, but the red glow from inside the white fog got brighter. Lexie could feel the heat now, heat pouring from the creature's mouth. Heat that rolled through the room. Heat so intense, it sucked air out of the room.

Lexie raised the document. The creature's red eyes flickered and its head moved just a little toward the document.

Aloud, Lexie recited the last sentence of the spell again. The banishing line. Her voice was deep enough she barely recognized it. She poured power into the spell, adding what she could of herself to make this work.

The creature started toward the circle, a slow-moving rush of fog and heat and that silent, horrifying scream. The silence hurt Lexie's ears almost as much as sound would.

She raised the document higher. "Get ready," she said to Miles.

The creature lunged toward the circle, the fog spreading out around the base, the red glow obliterating the light from Lexie's magic. Its jaw unhinged further. Heat blasted them, close enough to burn, and the creature's wings swept through the air, churning the heat and fog into a chaos she could no longer see through.

Lexie lurched backward toward the fire, her gaze on the creature.

The creature flapped its wings harder and the air outside the circle whipped up the furniture and few possessions in the room. Knocked over the table. Bottles off the shelves crashed to the wooden floor. The stench of rot filled the closed space, making Lexie gag. And Miles bent over, his hands on his knees, as if he would throw up.

Lexie glanced back at the fire, then at the creature, at the hurricane swirl of debris it churned up, then down at her circle's edge.

She broke her circle with a foot across the salt and chalk. And threw the document into the flames.

The fire roared high into the chimney, as sound swept through the cabin. Screaming. Moaning. Howling. Horror filled screeches and wails.

Lexie dropped to her knees, clamping her hands over her ears.

The storm of debris flew around the room, a swirling circle of chaos and deadly shards of wood and glass. The noise echoed off the enclosed space so loudly, Lexie saw spots.

In the fireplace, the document floated inside the flames. Not burning.

The howl of anger and fear and grief covered her, a smothering blanket. She could barely breathe. Wondered if her heart was still working. Felt the creature's heat start to burn her skin.

She'd failed. The document wasn't burning. She and Miles were going to die.

Even as that thought crossed her mind, a pair of strong arms wrapped around her, sending her crashing backward against the hard wooden floor. She looked up in time to see the creature flying overhead, racing toward the three hundred year old fire…

Plunging into the flames.

As the document…

Burned.

She had to blink a few times to take that in. The old parchment curled at the edges, blackening, as flames caught and poked through the center of the page. Spreading fast. Consuming it.

The creature filled up the fireplace now, thrashing and screaming. But the sound no longer pierced Lexie's brain. As the document burned, the creature grew smaller. And smaller. The fog and red that had made up its body faded, dissipated. Until only the glowing eyes remained. As the last of the document turned black and charred, as the last pieces of parchment burned to ash, the red eyes swirled in a strange sort of pattern.

And then winked out.

The storm of debris around them died suddenly, the instant the eyes vanished. Everything clattered to the floor in a rain of broken wood and glass. Lexie ducked, and Miles covered her with his own body. When the noise stopped, they both turned to look at the fire.

For a long moment, they lay on the hard floor, watching as the flames settled back into their normal flickering.

Then that, too, started to shrink.

Lexie didn't move, barely breathed, as they watched the more than three hundred year old fire slowly, slowly die down.

Finally, with no ceremony or noise, the flames went out.

And plunged the cabin into darkness.

CHAPTER EIGHT

The blue-white glow of light from Lexie's magic slowly re-illuminated the cabin interior. She blinked a few times as her eyes adjusted. She wasn't even sure when her light spell had broken and gone out in all the chaos, but having that glow of her own magic chasing away the shadows allowed her to take her first full breath in what felt like hours.

"Are you okay?" Miles asked, sitting up.

She realized he'd still had his arms around her as they'd huddled on the floor together.

She sat up next to him, assessing herself. There was a thin slice on her bicep, red but not bleeding. Another cut on her jaw that was bleeding a little, but not bad. And some sore spots on her hip and elbow she thought would probably show up as purple bruises before long. Her bag was scrunched under her, so she adjusted it, letting the strap settle into a less restricted position across her chest. Her ear drums hadn't burst—that had seemed like a possibility in the middle of the chaos—but there was a ringing in her ear from the sudden silence.

Otherwise… "I think I'm fine. Nothing that won't heal. You?"

"Same. A few bruises." He touched his ear and his fingers came away with a little blood. "Few cuts. But I can move and breath so none of it is too bad."

She sighed and sent up a silent *thank you* to the goddess.

"Did it work?" Miles asked, looking around.

The cabin was a mess now. Furniture shattered into shards of wood. The contents of the shelves broken, their putrid contents spilling out.

Lexie saw that and winced. "We should get out of here. There's no telling what sort of toxins were released from those bottles."

They helped each other climb to their feet and then stumbled to the cottage door. But they both paused on the threshold to look back. The fireplace was cold and empty. Not even ash from the document remained. No glowing eyes. No fog. Except for the wrecked furniture, and the stench of whatever had been in those bottles, the room looked…empty.

"Feels empty," Miles said.

Lexie nodded.

They left the cottage, and Miles locked the door behind them as they stood in the strange corridor outside. The weird, oppressive feeling had faded. Lexie wasn't sure if that was just her own relief to be out of the cottage or a real shift in the house.

They started back through the maze of strangely shaped hallways and rooms, returning without discussing it to the Victorian sitting room. On the way, Miles paused long enough at a bathroom to collect some gauze, wet wipes, antibacterial gel, and band-aids, which made Lexie smile.

They cleaned up their various cuts while sitting on the

delicate-looking couch in the Victorian sitting room, not talking much until after the last band-aid had been applied.

Then Miles sat back and glanced around the room. "Might be relief we didn't die, but… The place feels different to me now."

"Not as…oppressive," she said. "Not so much like its closing in around us."

"That's it. It's not closing in around me and leaving me dizzy anymore." He nodded. "Feels… Not sure how to say this. Feels more…open?"

She got it. It wasn't that the house didn't still *look* strange. But that *feeling* of it glaring at them and holding them here seemed to have shifted.

"You think you can leave without getting forced back now?" she asked quietly.

He met her gaze. "Let's find out."

He took her hand and led her through the strangely-sized hallway, back to the front door. A long moment passed as he stood staring at the doorknob, still holding her hand. Lexie gave his a little squeeze. And he opened the door.

When they were outside, in the still surprisingly bright, sunny afternoon, the autumn chill crisp and dry, Miles held himself perfectly still, his back to the house.

Then suddenly he took in a deep deep breath. Let it out in a whoosh.

He blinked down at her. "I feel…normal. At least I think this is normal. I haven't felt this way since inheriting the house. The… The tie that kept forcing me back here, that stretched feeling whenever I left… That's not there anymore."

"It worked."

"I think it worked." He smiled. And then he laughed.

And then to Lexie surprised, he grabbed her up into a hug

that lifted her off her feet. The gesture startled a laugh from her, and she hugged him back.

"Thank you," he said, when he put her back on her feet. He framed her face with his hands and held her gaze. "Thank you."

She smiled. "Glad I could help."

"I owe you a dinner. And many drinks. And a car."

Another chuckle. "I don't need the car. But I will take the dinner and drinks."

He grinned, a look so unexpectedly charming, Lexie had to blink. She thought him handsome before, but that grin…

He grabbed her hand again and walked her across the circular driveway in front of the house to her waiting rental car. "There's a restaurant in Salem, a place I've been wanting to go but haven't had the energy." He shivered a little. "Any food restrictions?" he asked as he held the driver's side door for her to slide in.

She smiled at the gesture. "So long as it's not a fish place, I'm good."

"No fish?"

"No fish," she said.

"Good. I hate fish, too." He tapped her door as he closed it gently, then practically bounced around to the passenger's side of the car.

Lexie stared back at the house as she waited for Miles to climb in. It still looked as strange and awkward and odd as it had when she'd arrived. But that feeling of strangeness was gone. It was just an architectural oddity now.

She patted her bag, the leather journal inside with all her notes on the original owner of the cabin. She'd have to finish filling in some details later. But after dinner. And maybe after a good night sleep.

In the woods to the right of the house, she thought she

caught something flash. When she looked, she didn't see anything. Maybe just some sunlight flickering off leaves? A sense of peace settled over her as she looked, though.

A sense that finally, finally she could rest.

The passenger door closed with a gentle thud. "Ready?" Miles said, all bright smiles and enthusiasm as he buckled his seatbelt. "I'm starving now."

She smiled and put the car into gear. Looking forward to a nice, quiet dinner with a handsome man. Who was no longer a prisoner to his ancestor's house.

An evening, and an ending, she could live with.

Enjoy all of the
Haunts
and Howls
Collections

Out Now!

EXCERPT FROM BONE
LANTERN WITCH

CHAPTER 1

*A*ngela Jordan fingered her pentagram bracelet and stared at the natural V-shape formed by the split trunk of the small oak tree. She'd tried not to look, had managed to avoid looking on accident for years. But this tree sitting innocuously along the path from the Mosholu entrance in the New York Botanical Gardens had caught her off guard.

Or maybe her guard was down because of why she was here.

She rubbed the dangling silver pentagram charm in slow clockwise circles, pressing into the pattern with each pass over the top of the dime-sized disk. She took a step toward the tree. A slight tremor from the charm stopping her. The scent of sulfur and heat burned her nostrils, a sharp contrast with the cool autumn air. Ordinary, mundane humans walked behind her on the paved path, ignoring her, unable to see the horror she watched between the oak's trunk.

They were all so luckily innocent, she thought, as a demon from the hellscape noticed her.

She froze. Even her fingers stilled on the pentagram. Her

heartbeat pounded. Panic she hadn't felt in months rushed through her blood stream.

If she could just stay still enough, maybe it wouldn't realize she could see it, maybe it wouldn't know.

The creature swiveled its head and flicked the air with its forked tongue, its red-eyed gaze narrowing. Its skin was the color of rolling volcanic lava, hard sections of black covered its chest and thighs, under that a luminous red and yellow glow. It hissed, though she couldn't hear the sound yet, revealing rows of shark-sharp teeth.

She tried to swallow without making any movements, not while it was looking at her. She failed.

The demon raced across the burning, charred land. Charging her. Barreling toward the rip she'd created between its realm and hers. It ran on all fours, even though it was vaguely human shaped, its spiked tail high behind it.

A lesser fire beast. Not the same species exactly. Not the same one as that night.

But the same hellscape.

The same realm.

She held her ground, unable to move even if she'd wanted to, glued by panic and fears she'd worked for almost two years to overcome. The stink of sulfur intensified, along with the burning smell of oak. Ash coated her tongue. An illusion she couldn't ignore.

The demon hit the tree and reached through the split in the trunk, grasping hands tipped with impossibly long claws stretched toward her. She could hear its screams now, so high-pitched the sound ripped across her nerves, piercing and sharp. Its mouth stretched and distorted with its cries, taking shapes no being of this realm could manage.

Laughter and the chatter of a child moved behind her. The real world. Oblivious to the nightmare trying to reaching them. They'd see it if it got out, if any of the beasts escaped. The humans would see it.

And they'd know she let it free.

Angie folded her hand around her pentagram charm, encompassing the white beads of the bracelet itself where it hung loosely around her wrist. The charm burned coldly in her palm, the sensation a reassuring jolt of reality and sanity. A soft breeze moved through her hair, ruffling the baby hairs on her forehead, making her hanging moon earrings tinkle lightly.

Unless she was working, she didn't wear the stereotypical trappings of a psychic and witch. Not what mundane humans expected. No flowing skirts and excessive silver jewelry. No braids or patchouli-scented perfume. Today, she wore her comfortable camouflage—jeans and a t-shirt, hiking boots and a light autumn jacket. Only the pentagram bracelet, which she never risked taking off, and the earrings—a present from her brothers to represent her love of astronomy more than her witchy gifts—even hinted at her lineage.

None of it revealed her most horrible skill.

The sounds of the demon's screams got louder, a hissing and screeching that raised the hair on her arms. Behind it, more demons noticed the breach. Noticed her. They piled against the thin barrier, pushing through the V made by the oak's trunk like a writhing mass of snakes about to spill into this world.

A tug on Angie's jacket made her breath catch. She sucked in cool air, swallowed her screech, and glanced down.

A little girl, maybe five or six years old, looked up at her with wide eyes and a shy smile. Angie heard the screams of protest from the oak, the sounds piercing her skull. She smiled at the little girl in her unicorn t-shirt and pink ballerina skirt. The gold plastic crown tucked into her tightly curled black hair glittered in the autumn sunlight.

When the girl tugged Angie's jacket again, Angie bent lower so she was eye level with the child, moving her big purse to one side so it wouldn't get in the way.

"Are you a model?" the girl asked, her whisper not very quiet.

Angie chuckled. "No," she said. "Are you?"

The girl giggled and bounced on her toes. "I'm gonna be," she confided. "But right now I'm a princess."

"Yeah you are," Angie said. "And a beautiful one at that."

The girl's mother spotted the conversation and hurried over. "Sorry," she said. "I hope she wasn't bothering you. She's convinced you're a model."

"No problem." Angie waved to the girl as her mother pulled her up the paved road toward the children's section of the gardens.

The scent of sulfur had faded, leaving only the faint spoiled-egg taste of it in Angie's mouth.

She glanced at the oak from the corner of her eye, not making the same mistake she'd made earlier. She could still see the faint glow of the hellscape beyond, but the barrier between realms had solidified.

No demons would be climbing through today.

She pushed her hair out of her face, letting the breeze cool the sweat at her temples. When she felt settled, she tugged her jacket sleeves down, covering her bracelet, though she curled her fingers up into the sleeve to brush the charm one last time. She adjusted her purse at her hip, straightening the strap over her shoulder and across her chest.

Then, letting the fresh scents of green grass, damp earth, and the faint smell of hot sauce from the food truck at the front of the gardens clear out her senses, she moved on, studiously ignoring all the natural Vs formed in the trunks of trees.

Angie met him at the pavilion in the decorative conifers section of the gardens. Here, dozens of varieties of pines filled the rolling hills, scenting the air. Angie loved conifers. Very few of them grew with split trunks.

"How many times do I have to tell you I'm not doing this anymore," she said as she approached the loan man sitting inside the gray stone pavilion.

The open top let light spill across his face, making him look younger than his almost forty-three years. His short dark hair was still free of any hint of gray, his brown skin smooth, no creases or laugh lines around his dark brown eyes or full mouth. Sometime in the last year, he'd gone from clean shaven to a dark mustache and goatee-style beard, also without any gray.

Sebastian was a demon hunter, though, and they never looked their age. It wouldn't matter if he was forty-three or sixty-three or even eighty-three. Demon hunters remained exactly the age they wanted to stay. They willed away the process of aging the way they willed away demons called to this realm.

A demon hunter's will was an awesome thing to behold. A rare trait in humans, that kind of will. Rarer still that innate skill put to good use. And it was a trait fewer and fewer possessed with each passing year. Still, there were enough to keep the demon realms at bay. For now. It was their job to fight the fights and keep this world blissfully unaware of the threat.

At least, most people were blissfully unaware.

She refocused on Sebastian. He wore jeans and a burnt

orange sweater that served to both honor the season and show off his broad shoulders and strong physique. The color suited him. Even without the softening glow of the afternoon sunlight, he would look good, though. A gorgeous, stunning man in his prime.

Her chest ached. She ignored it.

As she sat next to him, cradling her overlarge faux-leather purse in her lap, she reminded herself, again, demon hunting was his job. *Not* hers.

He studied her, his head tilted to one side as his gaze traveled over her face, lingering on her eyes, her lips. "You're looking good, Ang," he said, his voice deep, the English accent prominent.

She gestured at the surrounding trees, ignoring the compliment and the way his voice always sent a little tingle along her spine. "The Botanical Gardens was an interesting choice. Unless we're here for a specific reason. Either way, the answer is no."

He grinned, quick and sudden, an expression that gave him a boyish charm. That smile had always gotten her into trouble. "Maybe I just wanted to see you again," he said.

"If that were the case, we could have met for a coffee in a crowded café in the city. No reason to get me out here where no one will overhear our conversation."

"I could have kept anyone from overhearing our conversation even in a crowded café," he reminded her.

"We both know you didn't call me for a friendly reunion." Unfortunately. She swallowed that response. "Or anything else personal. We both know this is business."

In the first six months after they'd broken up, when she'd been determined to be done with demon hunting because it had nearly killed her, he'd come to her several times in New York, trying to coax her back into his world. She'd made the mistake of following him into two more hunts before she'd put her foot down for good. Two more hunts she should never have been involved in after…

She let out a long breath. "I'm not dealing in your business anymore. I can't do it again, Sebastian. I can't."

His smile dropped away. "I wouldn't ask if it wasn't necessary. I don't like putting you through this any more than you like going through it."

She snorted. "Right. Which is why you keep dragging me back in."

She'd been trying to put the demon world behind her for almost two years. She'd worked hard to settle into a life without demons and hunters. Or at least, she'd tried to.

She hadn't seen Sebastian in a year and a half, after yet another hunt went horribly wrong for her. She'd finally, finally demanded he not contact her again unless it was an emergency. The last year and a half had been one of the most peaceful, uneventful times in her life. She'd loved it.

She wasn't going to give that up now, just because he flashed those gorgeous dark eyes at her. No matter how easy it was to ignore the hint of red in their depths. No matter how easy it was to fall back into the old ways, the old feelings.

"Ang," he said, drawing out her nickname. He held out his hand, palm up. "I tried to stay away. This time I really tried. But there's no one else like you in this world. And I need your help."

She let out a huff of a sigh and looked out over the trees, keeping her gaze on the solid trunk of a pine just down the hill from them. She'd known, when he texted her out of the blue, she'd known it would be something like this. Some demon related issue.

"No," she said without looking at him. She could still taste the sulfur and ash in her mouth from the earlier incident.

That realm… The reminder helped her hold firm. "No, Seb. No more. Not ever again."

"I told her you wouldn't want to be involved," Sebastian said quietly. "I had to ask."

"Aidan?" Angie shook her head. "Of course."

Aidan was one of the oldest and most skilled demon hunters to walk this realm. No one was sure how old she was, or how long she'd been fighting demons. Just that she was still alive when so many others weren't. She was a legend among demon hunters. She was the hunter who'd found and trained Sebastian.

The hunter who'd rescued Angie from herself.

"You weren't her only option," Sebastian said. "Just a more straight-forward choice than any of the others left to us without you."

"I'm not going to ask," she said firmly, still not looking at him.

If she asked what the problem was, what they wanted her to do, she'd be halfway to giving in. She wouldn't be able to hear about the trouble and ignore it. He'd gotten her before with that trick. Better not to know. Better to stay ignorant and let the hunters handle it themselves.

"It's okay, Angie," he said, his voice quiet. "We'll save the child without you."

"You son of a bitch," she hissed. "Son of a bitch." She glared at him, her jaw tight. "I hate you for this."

He nodded. "I know."

"Bastard." She wrapped her fingers around the pentagram on her bracelet. "Tell me."

～

**Don't miss Bone Lantern Witch
Book one in the Demon Witch series.
Out Now!**

BOOKS BY KAT SIMONS

Urban Fantasy

The Cary Redmond Series

Cary Redmond Short Stories

Demon Witch Series

Contemporary Fantasy

Haunts and Howls Collections

Joan of Kerry Series

Tombstone Wizard

The Unshattered Sword

Destiny Through the Cats Eyes

Going Out of Business: Everything's for Sale

Paranormal Romance

Tiger Shifters Series

Romancing the Leopard: A Tiger Shifters-Cary Redmond Crossover Novel

The Seven Families Series: Wolf Clan

Coming soon in 2023

Contemporary Romances

Designed for You

Poinsettias and Possibilities

Coming December 2022

Mystery and Thriller

Galileo's Pendulum

Coming November 2022

ABOUT THE AUTHOR

Kat Simons earned her Ph.D. in animal behavior, working with animals as diverse as dolphins and deer. She brought her experience and knowledge of biology to her paranormal romance and urban fantasy fiction, where she delights in taking nature and turning it on its ear. She writes urban fantasy, contemporary fantasy, and paranormal romance in series which combine action adventure, the otherworldly, and a frequent dose of sexy romance.

The latest book in her bestselling romantic urban fantasy series about Protector Cary Redmond, THE TROUBLE WITH DEATH AND DEMON GODS, is out now. As are the newest stories in the romantic urban fantasy Demon Witch series, including the first "meet cute" for Angie and her demon hunter boyfriend Sebastian in the novella HOWLING DREADFUL. Readers can also expect a brand new paranormal romance series from Kat in 2023.

For something a little different, Kat also publishes fantasy, science fiction, and the occasional hockey romance under the name Isabo Kelly (https://www.isabokelly.com).

After traveling the world, living in places like Hawaii, Germany, and Ireland, Kat now lives in New York City with her family and a library's worth of books.

The Cary Redmond Series

Out Now!

Don't miss the latest Kat Simons
news, updates, excerpts, cover reveals
and more!

All New Subscribers get two exclusive stories:

Mate Run
A Tiger Shifters paranormal romance short story

and

When Cary Met Ariel
A Cary Redmond urban fantasy novella

Join Now!

https://bit.ly/KatSimonsNewsletter